BLAKE'S BRIDE

SEVEN BRIDES FOR SEVEN BROTHERS
BOOK FOUR

KATHLEEN LAWLESS

ISBN ebook: 978-1-9990635-0-4

ISBN print: 978-1-989873-52-6

Seven Brides for Seven Brothers **Reviews**

What reviewers are saying about the *Seven Brides for Seven Brothers* series...

"GREAT SERIES!!!" Top 500 reviewer

"If you have not picked up the series, do yourself a favor, you will be glad you do."

"I loved the continuity in the series—and the resolution"

"Sweet and romantic."

"This entire series is going into my library to be read again and again."

"I just love reading Kathleen's books—they keep me coming back for more."

If you haven't already done so, sign up for my VIP Reader's Newsletter and be the first to hear about free books, fan-priced sales, and my new series. Details at the end of the book.

CHAPTER 1

It was a perfect day for a wedding. The park's gazebo was decked in yards and yards of ribbon, while the shiny white posts were adorned with sprays of wild flowers. Rows of benches next to chairs borrowed from the café offered guests a spot to sit. Smack in the center of the gazebo, the seven Mason brothers waited in a straight line.

Storm, alongside her fellow bridesmaid, Amanda, wiped her sweaty palm on the skirt of her frock and clutched her nosegay tightly. This was her first time being a bridesmaid. It was also her first time in such a fancy dress, edged in lace and all, crafted by her own hand.

From her vantage point, Storm watched Henrietta, the bride, appear on the arm of her long-time friend Percival Bloom. Slowly, the duo made their way across the park to the gazebo where Braydon Mason, the groom, waited along with the reverend and the wedding party. Before today, Storm had never seen the normally confident Braydon Mason look nervous.

As the ceremony got underway, Storm snuck a subtle glance at Blake Mason, flanked by his brothers. Laura

Mason, the first Mason bride, and now with child, had confided that Blake had a secret. Storm could relate to secrets. She had a few of her own. If only her "big" secret was as innocent as Blake's. Lots of folks out west couldn't read. As a librarian, she was no stranger to witnessing their struggles, and happy when she was able to help.

Blake's situation was a bit different, and Storm didn't know if she could help him or not, but she had promised Laura she would try.

She pulled her attention back to the ceremony, just as Braydon moved in to kiss his bride. Dark-haired Henrietta, who folks around town had grown used to seeing in clothing that looked more like a man's shirt and trousers than ladies' attire, made a beautiful bride. Henrietta looked so happy as she gazed at her handsome groom, the way every bride ought to.

After the ceremony, a wagonload of food was hauled to the park from the café and set out on long trestle tables shaded by the canvas covering. Wedding guests quickly lined up and filled their plates. A keg of beer was tapped and the gents eagerly lined up to quench their thirst. Storm had only been calling on Bullet with her mobile library for a short time, but her arrival marked the first time she remembered feeling truly safe since she and her father emigrated from Ireland to New York City. Thankfully, here in Arizona, New York felt like it was two lifetimes away. The second nightmare lifetime also lay behind her, far away in Colorado.

"What's a wedding without Champagne?" Percy, who had given away the bride, approached and offered her one of the two glasses he carried. "Now that our roles are fulfilled, it's time to relax and enjoy ourselves."

Storm fought back the old familiar fears that assailed

her whenever a man got too close. She had nothing to be afraid of here in Bullet. And Percy's manner of speech reminded her a tiny bit of her home, even though British and Irish accents were very different from each other. Faking a comfortable smile, she clinked her glass against Percy's. "To the bride and groom."

"To the bride and groom," Percy repeated.

Storm took her first ever sip of Champagne, and found it not at all what she expected. She could almost feel the bubbles dance along the tip of her tongue. It tasted like sunshine in a glass. She was about to say as much to Percy, then stopped. Her companion was clearly no stranger to exotic wines, or foods, or places, the way she was. She asked, instead, "Did you ever think you'd see this day? Henrietta married?"

Percy choked on his Champagne. "Truthfully? No." He glanced to where the happy couple stood chatting with their guests. "But she may well have found the one man able to keep her interested. And in line." He softened his words with a fond smile.

Did women really find men interesting? Rather than someone to fear? Someone bigger and stronger and more powerful, who could turn against a woman in seconds. Storm pondered the unfamiliar concept.

"On a much different note," Percy continued, "I must confess to being curious as to how you got your unusual name."

Storm smiled, recalling the story her da had oft repeated. "According to my da, my ma wanted to name me Maureen after her ma. Da didn't get along with her mother and figured if I was a boy that would be the end of it. Apparently, the night I was born Ireland was rocked with a ferocious storm, the worst one in over a hundred years. Because of that, Da managed to convince Ma it was God's way of choosing my name. So Storm I am."

"But not Stormy your temperament," Percy said.

"I do have the Irish temper," Storm said. "I've learned over the years to control it." Uncomfortable talking so much about herself, she turned the conversation back to Percy. "I gather you and Henrietta have had quite the adventures over the years, hunting treasure."

"I'll miss her," Percy said simply. He gave Storm a probing glance. "How about you? Are you planning to linger here in Bullet for much longer?"

"I'm not sure yet. Amanda is talking about building some sort of town hall with room for a permanent library. If she does, she wants me to help her set it up."

Percy eyed her seriously over the rim of his glass. "Be careful, Storm. Bullet and its townsfolk have a way of subtly wrapping their tentacles around you, cloaking you in comfort and familiarity, until you don't want to leave."

The very idea stabbed her with fresh fear. "Has that happened to you yet?"

"Merciful heavens, no." Percy drained his glass, and stared at it as if wondering how it became empty so quickly. "Time for a refill."

Up at the gazebo where the ceremony had taken place, Storm saw a trio of musicians setting up their instruments. Perhaps, after the wedding waltz, she would be free to make her escape.

Across the way, she saw Laura Mason beckoning to her. No one could say "no" to Laura, especially with her being in a family way. Storm hurried toward Laura and arrived just as Brody, Laura's husband, was preparing to leave. "I'm going to get Laura a plate. Can I get you anything, Storm?"

"No, thank you." Storm pressed her lips together. Brody

Mason was a nice man, the head of the Mason brothers' clan. She had to stop reading ulterior motives into things every time a man spoke to her.

Laura patted the empty seat next to her. "Did you have a chance to talk to Blake yet?" As Storm sat, Laura lowered her voice so no one near them could hear what she was saying.

"Not yet." Already Storm was regretting her offer to try and help Blake learn to read. She had only met a few people in her travels who were word blind, and fewer still who eventually managed to overcome the affliction in order to read and write simple words.

She twisted her hands together. She knew what it was like to be different. She'd never forget the nuns in Ireland, rapping her knuckles painfully with their rosary beads or a ruler, forcing her to write with her right hand, when holding a pencil in her left had felt far more natural.

"Well, there he is, all alone over there." Laura gave her a tiny push. "Now's your chance."

Head high, Storm nodded and rose, reminding herself it was important she maintain control. In every aspect of her life. Particularly when it came to men.

If Blake saw her coming, he pretended not to, turning to look in the opposite direction of the park. "Laura said I should come ask you to dance," she said, faking a confidence she was far from feeling. If Blake rejected her, she could at least tell Laura she had tried. "Seeing as how she'll soon be too big to dance herself, I think she's living vicariously through the rest of us."

Her sympathy rose. Poor Blake reminded her of a trapped animal, eyes sliding from side to side as if seeking escape.

"Weddings make me uncomfortable too," she confided.

"You, at least, have had some practice lately, what with three of your brothers tying the knot in the last short while. Do you fellows really build a new cabin for each couple on the ranch?"

"Yes, ma'am." Blake swallowed thickly, his Adam's apple bobbing with the movement. "I'm afraid I'm not much of one on the dance floor, Miss Storm."

"Good." She took his arm. "Neither am I. Two left feet, I believe is the expression."

She schooled herself not to freeze up or flinch when she put her hand into Blake's and felt his other hand tentatively rest on her waist. It seemed easier knowing he was at least as uncomfortable as she was.

"Did the groom really make a wager with you and your brothers that he would win over Henrietta and have her eating out of his hand?"

Blake smiled down at her, and she saw his eyes light up in an appealing way with the memory. "Things got real interesting once Henrietta found out and turned the tables on him. She did it so fast he never knew what hit him."

His smile was catching, and Storm traded her sigh for a smile of her own. Blake was lucky to have the type of close family ties that she herself had never known.

"Henrietta is one smart lady," Storm said. "Speaking of smart, Laura said you're the one I should talk to."

"I'm not smart," Blake said, his smile fading. "You want to talk to Brody or the twins for smart."

"You're the one Laura said could help me out. She told me you're really good with tools. I require a few more book-shelves built into the mobile library. I also wanted to see about getting a permanent bed and some drawers built in the sleeping loft, so things aren't always sliding around when I'm traveling."

He blinked down at her. "Do you sleep in there?"

She nodded. "A lot of the small towns I travel to are like Bullet, and have no hotel. And no place a lady could stay on her own."

He frowned. "Doesn't sound like much of a life for a lady."

She raised her chin a notch. "Why? Just because I'm not slaving away on a farm somewhere with a bunch of brats hanging on my apron strings?" She shuddered as she spoke, recalling the life she had narrowly escaped.

Blake fell silent, as if deciding how much to share. "Never had a real home till I came here. Wouldn't trade it for anything."

"Consider yourself lucky. How did that all come about, anyway? You hooking up with Brody and the others."

His eyes took on a faraway look. "Brody was living with his uncle out at the ranch. Helped me out of a tight spot, and convinced me I should stay on." He shrugged. "So I did. Kind of my way of saying 'thanks'."

SOMEHOW, Storm made dancing seem easier than Blake remembered from the last two weddings, where he'd been forced to stomp around with a few of the town's hopeful spinsters. Seemed now that a couple of the brothers had tied the knot, the rest of them had become fair game.

The conversation between him and Storm had felt easy as well. By the time the musicians stopped for a break, Blake had found himself agreeing to swing by the mobile library sometime in the next few days and see what he could do.

Right now, it was past time for him to help the others keep an eye on things. Brody ought not be away from Laura's side for too long. Bradley and Amanda were still practically newlyweds. They sure acted like it, anyways, even though they'd been wed some few months now. Which left him and the twins and Benjamin to patrol the perimeter of the park and keep out any undesirables.

One never knew what crazy antics Hawkes might decide to pull.

Benjamin was the first one he came across. "Ready for a break?" he asked.

"Sure," Ben said. Brody often said Ben, the best gunman of the group, had been born with a gun in his hand. Revolver or rifle, the firearm had sure seemed like a natural appendage anytime Blake had seen him wield one.

"I'll go grab a bite. Is Georgina still around somewhere?"

"Think so." Georgina was the owner of the town's café. Last year she had expanded the facility, hired some extra help, and her business appeared to be going really well. He'd noticed lately that Georgina was looking a lot more gussied than she ever used to. He wondered if wedding bells might be chiming in Benjamin's future anytime soon. He'd come across the two of them chatting on more than one occasion, and the other man seemed to have a ready list of excuses to drop by the café.

"It's been pretty quiet," Ben said, his eyes scanning the area of the park that dipped down to the river, his hand never far from his revolver. "Still, I'd feel better if Braydon and Henrietta had agreed to have the wedding inside somewhere."

"There is nowhere big enough for the whole town, short of moving the wedding to Yuma," Blake said. "They weren't about to have their wedding in the café the way Bradley and Amanda did."

"I guess. And Brody getting married on the ranch didn't keep Hawkes from doing his bit to disrupt things."

"Way I see it," Blake said, "getting married just seems a whole lot more trouble than it's worth."

Ben grinned knowingly. "Don't tell me you're getting tired of building new cabins out at the ranch?"

Blake glanced down at his hands, fingertips ridged with calluses. "I like doing things with my hands. I just happen to prefer it when the things I'm working with have moving parts."

"Saw you dancing with Storm earlier. Lady appears to have a few moving parts of her own."

"That so?" Blake said, stiffly. "I hadn't noticed."

Ben ruffled his hair, a gesture Blake detested, even though he knew it was done with affection. "Don't be kidding a kidder, bro. She's a looker, that one. Little stand-offish, kinda like you."

Blake crossed his arms over his chest. "Hell, if I'm stand-offish!" But he knew there was a grain of truth to Benjamin's words. Even though he'd known Brody the longest, he still felt like an outsider, not as easy with the family camaraderie as the others.

Part of him had never quite gotten over being the runt in the orphanage, the one all the other kids bullied and called dummy when he couldn't master his sums or his letters. He sighed. A lot of good had come into his life since those early days, but being able to read and write still eluded him. He'd come to accept that that was the way things were. As Brody kept telling him, he had other talents.

If he could use those talents to help out a nice lady like Storm when she needed a hand, then he was happy to help.

Moving away from the distraction of the music and gaiety behind him, Blake patrolled the edge of the park near where it met the riverbank. He was relieved to see no signs of intruders or furtive movement down near the river's edge, and was fixing to go back when he saw a small wooden crate, half-hidden in the tall, straw-colored grass. He squatted down for a closer look. It looked like something was leaking from the box. A foreign, oily-looking substance.

Blake felt the hair rise on the back of his neck, coupled with an internal warning he couldn't ignore. The crate looked new, not something that had been suffering the weather for a while. He'd seen them working on the railroad and knew they'd used some powerful explosives to blast through rock.

The crate was stamped with a bunch of squiggles that Blake thought must be the name of the company. He recognized the letter 'B' because he knew that was what his name started with. Gingerly, he picked up the crate and rose, careful not to get any leakage on his good wedding suit.

"What's that you've got?"

His mouth went dry when he looked up to see Storm picking her way toward him, her skirt swishing softly against the tall, dry grass. It sounded loud as a drum roll.

His words came out, rusty-sounding with fear. "Don't come any closer."

"Blake?" She hesitated where she stood, her eyes worried.

He spoke slowly and measured. "Turn around slow. Go back the way you came. Walk slow and careful. And don't say anything to anyone else. Got it?"

She eyed the crate. "Is that what I think it is?"

His arms started to ache from more than just the weight he held. He held strong. He dared not move, not breathe too loud, just silently telegraphed the danger, his eyes to hers.

He had to give her credit. She did exactly as he asked. No

theatrics. No panic. Just backed away slowly, her eyes never leaving his.

Once she was out of sight, he took slow and carefully measured steps toward the river bank. Should any sudden movement accidentally detonate the crate of dynamite he held, he was a goner. He paused, steps from the edge of the river, said a prayer and heaved the crate for all he was worth.

It hit the surface of the water and had barely sunk from sight in an eddy of ripples when he heard a muffled explosion. The nearby ground shook and a sheet of water, like a geyser, flew straight into the air, droplets making it to land and raining on his head and shoulders.

Blake's shoulders slumped in relief. He hissed out a breath and dusted off his shaking hands. Impossible to know if the crate had been placed there deliberately, or somehow fell off the back of a delivery wagon. And maybe nothing would have happened if he hadn't disturbed it. On the other hand ...

Moments later, Barron and Bishop, the twins, came loping his way, with Storm on their heels.

"What the hell—" This from Barron. He knew it was Barron because of the blue shirt he wore. Whenever the twins dressed in identical clothing he was in trouble.

"Saw a suspicious box," Blake said with a shrug.

"Explosives," Bishop said.

"So it would seem."

"You shouldn't have touched it," Barron said.

"Too late for that." The rest of what he was thinking stayed unspoken. He didn't care much about his own safety, but when it came to everyone else, he would gladly make any sacrifice to keep his family safe. His pathetic life had never felt very worthwhile.

That fateful day when Brody's path crossed his, he'd

been wishing the bullies beating him would just kill him and get it over with. Save him the trouble. Instead, Brody had scooped him up, given him something to live for.

"I think you were very brave," Storm chimed in.

Her words barely registered. It was less bravery, and more the care he had for others. He straightened, newly aware he had done something to be proud of. No one had ever told him before that he was brave.

"Here comes the cavalry," said Bishop, as Brody and Bradley came bearing down on them.

Quickly Blake explained what had happened. Brody issued orders to the others to scour the entire park and surrounding streets, keeping an eye out for anything suspicious.

"Are the guests doing okay?" Blake asked.

"Luckily the music muffled the worst of it. But when I felt the ground shaking, I knew something was up." Brody gave Blake a hard look. "What were you thinking? You could have been killed."

Blake looked away. Brody knew too much. "I just hope there's no more explosives around," he said. "Think we should close down the party early?"

"You can't!" Storm said.

"And let Hawkes win this round? Not a chance," Brody said.

Together, the three of them rejoined the festivities. Blake saw the way Brody's gaze circled the wedding guests, ever wary. Blake hated that they had to be on watch all the time. Especially on a day like today, which should be nothing but a joyous celebration.

Next to him, Storm spoke up. "I heard several guests explain it off as possibly distant thunder, even though we're months away from monsoon season."

"Let's stick to that." Apparently satisfied all was in order, Brody left them to go check on his wife.

Blake was still searching the crowd, looking for anything or anyone out of place. "Do you know who that fellow is over there?" He pointed out a newcomer dressed in city clothes, over near the gazebo.

"That's some newspaper reporter Henrietta mentioned. He's been following a story on treasure-hunting. Angling for an interview with Percy and Henrietta."

Blake grunted. Reporters with their newspaper stories was just one more reminder of what he missed out on by not being able to read. "He's going to have to move fast to talk to Henrietta before her and Braydon leave for Argentina."

"I still can't believe Braydon talked her into going. And neither can she. Did you know Henrietta hasn't seen her family since she left nearly ten years ago?"

"I'm willing to bet it's been longer than that for you," Blake said. "You have only the barest trace of Irish left in your voice."

She nodded, eyes wide and full of emotion. "I'm an orphan, Blake. Just like you."

Hawkes glowered at the way Don Lucas strode into his house as if he owned the place. Fancy clothes and title or not, a greaser was still a greaser. It was a sad state of affairs when a man had no choice but to make a deal with the devil, in this case Lucas, in order to achieve his goals.

"My men tell me you were at the train depot yesterday. Helped yourself to a crate from one of my shipments. You know those are all designated for projects I have planned."

"Don't get your knickers in a twist," Hawkes said. "You wouldn't have a bead on any of those projects if it wasn't for me."

"True or not, I find myself losing patience. I fear you are being bested, sidetracked in fact, by your vendetta with the Masons."

"Them low-borns are in my way. Our way," he corrected himself.

"And I've told you before. Strategy is everything when one is playing to win."

~

STORM'S WORDS had burned their way into Blake's brain. An orphan. He swore he'd seen a glimpse of unshed tears when she said it out loud, even though any hint of moisture vanished the second she blinked.

Those words, along with the woman who spoke them, stirred something deep within Blake. Something he'd never felt before. Until now, his emotions had been limited.

Fear and hatred.

Hatred and fear.

The fear was a holdover from his youth, from his life being in danger every single day until he no longer cared about living. Lately, any fear he felt had been for the members of his growing family. He feared for their safety, their happiness, their well-being.

The hatred had taken seed the day Hawkes had killed the twins' brother. He'd never before witnessed such pure evil. Evil he knew would stop at nothing to destroy the only people Blake had ever called family.

Yet, since Storm arrived in town, he recognized a differ-ence in himself. The world no longer appeared so unforgivingly black and white. He detected colors, colors represented with light and dark shades, bringing with them enough recognizable shades of light to help to chase away the darkness in his soul.

Storm turned to him. "I think we owe it to ourselves to have another dance."

And to his surprise, Blake found himself agreeing.

STORM COULD HAVE KICKED herself the second the words left her mouth. What was she thinking, asking Blake Mason to dance? He'd already promised to come by and take a look at the book wagon for her, step one in the scheme Laura had suckered Storm in on.

Looking up at him as he shuffled her clumsily around the dance floor, her heart went out to him. She knew, from the little Laura had told her, that Blake had had a tough childhood. Yet look at him today, so strong and handsome. And brave! His actions earlier had to be the bravest thing she had ever seen, the way he risked his own life to ensure the safety of others.

She found herself moving closer, resting her head against his chest, feeling the reassuring beat of his heart below her ear. She closed her eyes and pretended this was her life now. Safe in the arms of a man who would cherish and protect her.

She was so caught up in the sweetness of the moment, she didn't even notice when the music stopped. Belatedly she realized Blake had slowed to a stop. His grip loosened. She glanced around. Mercy, everyone else had left the dance floor. She released Blake and stepped back a pace.

"Sorry," she said. "I just ... I just ..."

His smile was back, light and teasing. "I know I can bore the ladies, not being much of a talker, but I've never had anyone fall asleep on me before."

"You're not boring, Blake. I thank you for the dance."

Swiftly, without looking back, she left the festivities behind her. It wouldn't do for her to get too comfortable here in Bullet or anyplace else. She had to keep moving. Make sure *he* didn't find her.

CHAPTER 2

Blake stared at the door on the rear of the oversize wooden book wagon parked on an empty chunk of land in town. Was one supposed to knock on a wagon like one would at the front door of a house? Feeling ridiculous, he clambered up the ladder-like steps and pounded with one fist.

When there was no response, he felt a wave of reprieve. Storm wasn't here. He'd stopped by like he'd promised. Obligation fulfilled. He turned to leave but got no farther. For there she was, smiling and waving from the other side of the road.

His heart gave a lurch, remembering how it had felt to put his hand on her waist when they were dancing at the wedding. Today she was dressed in a blue gingham dress, with a jaunty red hat perched atop her head. Her arms were full of books.

Gentlemanly manners he hadn't been aware he possessed, surfaced and propelled him to her side where he relieved her of the burden in her arms.

She smiled gratefully. "I'm so glad I didn't miss you. I wondered when you might be stopping by."

"Had some free time," he said, feeling unaccountably tongue-tied.

"Perfect timing. I'm leaving tomorrow." She pulled an iron key from her pocket and unlocked the door as she spoke.

"You're leaving?"

"Folks in some of the nearby towns will have finished the books they borrowed and be antsy for more."

Try as he might, he had no response. The squiggles on the pages of books he'd looked at over the years were just that, a bunch of lines and circles that made no sense, even when they weren't all jumbled together.

The inside of the wagon was barely tall enough for Storm to stand upright, and he had to duck his head to avoid giving his melon a good knock. From inside, he could see it had been an old buckboard, to which someone had added wood side walls and a roof.

And books. He'd never seen so many books at once, all different colors and sizes and shapes, spilling off the crowded shelves and filling boxes on the floor. Storm moved easily through the jumble as if it didn't exist.

For his part, Blake was conscious of their close confines, which heightened Storm's womanly fragrance as it wafted his way and stirred his senses. He wondered if she used a flower-scented soap to wash with.

"You read all these?"

Her laugh reminded him of music. "Heavens no. A lot of them aren't of any interest to me. But they will be to someone."

"How do you know how to find anything?" he asked.

"I have them loosely arranged by subject," she said.

"Non-fiction on that wall and fiction over there. Those are the dime novels at the end. People enjoy those." The interior smelled dusty, of old paper and leather, yet flowery at the same time. Maybe that scent came from the one lone plant. Dappled light filtered in from a glassed-in opening on the roof.

"Where did you get so many books?"

"I took over the book wagon from a lady I met when I was traveling south. She had arthritis so bad, she could barely manage the horses any longer. Since then, I've collected a lot more books. Most of them have been given to me by folks who are moving and don't have room to take them. They like what I'm doing around here. Folks who can afford it pay for a lending card. Those who can't," she shrugged. "I just give them one anyway."

"That's mighty generous of you."

"I don't need much to get by. Folks have been good to me. Some of them invite me for a meal when I'm in town. There's one blacksmith in a town up north. He borrows books and, in exchange, he shoes the horses for me."

"So it's not too lonely for you. Always moving from place to place."

"I didn't say that. Loneliness is something I think we all learn to deal with. At least part of the time."

She turned her big, dark eyes on him. "Laura asked Brody, and he said you could use some lumber they have at the ranch to make me shelves. I can't afford to pay much for your time."

"Don't want any pay," Blake mumbled. "Happy to help out." He pulled a length of string from the pocket of his shirt. He pointed. "This where you want those extra shelves?"

"Yes," she said. "And over there, if that's possible."

"What if I make you a wood cot, as well? Something that slides out of the way when you're not using it. And can be bolted to the floor so it stays put when you're driving."

"You can do that?" she said.

"Won't take much at all."

He stretched out the string and made markings on it with a lead pencil, aware of her eyes on him, watching every move.

"You remember what all those markings mean?" she said. "You don't write anything down?"

"Don't need to," he said. "I kind of take a picture of the area with my mind. Put that together with the marks. Works good for me."

For the first time ever, he didn't feel self-conscious for not using a numbered measuring stick like the others did when they were building something. His way was his way, and he didn't sense any ridicule from Storm because of it.

He rolled the string back up and tucked it in his pocket. "When you fixing to be back this way?"

"I think a week or ten days."

"I should have everything ready for you by then."

"So fast?" she said. "That's wonderful."

"Happy to help."

Measuring done, he couldn't find a ready excuse to linger any longer. "I guess I've kept you long enough from what you're doing."

"I'm the one who's keeping you," she said, as she preceded him back outside.

He paused near his horse. "You should come out to the ranch tonight for supper. It's the last night before Braydon and Henrietta leave for their trip."

"I don't want to impose on a family gathering," she said.

"Can't rightly speak for the others, but I'm willing to bet

the ladies would all be happy to see you. Poor Laura when she first married Brody— place was nothing but bachelor digs in those days."

"Well, I would like to talk to Amanda more about her plans here in town." Storm waved her arm to encompass the vacant land where they stood. "This is where she intends to build a town hall, part of which will have a dance hall area for lessons and plays and concerts. Like the one they have in Yuma."

"I've seen her and Laura in a huddle talking about stuff they want to do. Reckon that'll all change once they have a passel of young 'uns taking up their time."

Storm gave him a hard look. "Do you think Brody intends to quit ranching once he becomes a father?"

"'Course not," Blake said.

"So why would you expect Laura and Amanda to change their plans just because they have a family?"

Blake scuffed his toe in the dust. "I didn't mean it like that. Heck, I never had me a ma and a pa. What we got out there at the Copper Moon, that's everything I know about having a family."

"I have a feeling you'll be a very good uncle," Storm said. "And yes, I'd be happy to join you this evening."

HAWKES COULDN'T BELIEVE his ears when he heard that vacant parcel of land in town had got sold from underneath him. He'd every intention to purchase the land, just happened to be having some cash-flow difficulties of late. He figured he was safe waiting till he had the funds. Why would anyone want to own a piece of land that wasn't good for anything much besides another saloon or maybe a whore house?

He was still smarting from the way Zara had had him thrown out of her flea-bag place in Yuma. He knew exactly what this town needed. A saloon with some rooms upstairs where a man could take his ease at the end of the night. He envisioned himself in the role of taking the fillies for a test run. Don Lucas had a line on a band of greasers bringing young girls up from Mexico with promises of employment. Working on their backs with their legs spread.

He smiled at the thought, but his smile faded as he remembered the land was no longer up for grabs. That useless sheriff couldn't find out who was stupid enough to buy it. But Hawkes wouldn't rest until he found out who the new owner was. There were always ways to negotiate a new deal. And make sure the transaction weighed heavily in his favor.

IT WAS NOT without some trepidation that evening that Storm made her way to the Copper Moon ranch. She really enjoyed the Mason brides. She felt they were the first real friends she had made in a long time. But then there were the Mason brothers. All seven of them. Big and strong and intimidating. Well, not so much intimidating as she had first thought. Brody was kind and caring. She had learned a little of how he'd taken all the others under his wing and given them a home and family.

Blake was— She wasn't sure exactly what Blake was. She found him the least intimidating of the men. Which is one of the reasons she had agreed when Laura had asked if she might be able to help him learn to decipher letters and numbers. But still, she was more than a bit daunted at the thought of being under one roof with all of them, all that sheer male size and strength and energy.

Only the women were at the ranch house when she arrived, working in the kitchen together, looking as if they had been doing it all their lives rather than just a few months.

Henrietta particularly. Before she married Braydon, Henrietta had been a globe-trotting, treasure-hunting, independent female. Today she was pulling a pan of fresh-baked rolls from the oven and joking with the other women about married life. Storm wondered if Henrietta would be giving up her old life altogether, now that she was married to Braydon.

"Can I do something?" Storm asked, feeling like she was intruding on their easy camaraderie.

"Sit," Amanda said. "You're our guest. I am beyond thrilled Blake invited you tonight."

Storm shrugged. "I need to win his trust if I'm to help him with his ..." She paused delicately. "Challenges."

Amanda and Henrietta both turned her way. "Challenges?" they said in unison.

"Sorry." Storm sent an apologetic look toward Laura. "I didn't know they didn't know."

"Didn't know what?" Amanda asked.

"Blake's difficulty with reading," Laura said.

"Oh, that." Henrietta shrugged it off. "Not everyone is made for book-learning. Blake has other talents far more valuable. Do you know he' s working on a machine to stitch leather, so the others can fix all the bridles and chaps and even the saddles here on the ranch?"

"He's a love," Laura said. "So quiet and easy-going."

"I don't know," Amanda said. "I find him a bit difficult to get close to. He's pretty pulled back."

"Give him time," Laura said. "He's a little more reticent than the others."

Storm looked around. "Don't you three all have your own new homes and your own kitchens to cook in?"

"We do," Laura said. "But this way is more fun. One big, happy family. It makes Brody happy when we're all together, and a happy Brody—" She smiled the special smile of a woman well-loved. "Need I say more?"

"Where'd the boys go, anyway?" Henrietta asked. "I hope they're not off some place getting Braydon drunk. We leave tomorrow."

"How long will you be away?" Storm asked.

Henrietta shrugged. "Months, I expect."

"Are you excited?" Storm asked. Personally, she couldn't imagine returning to her homeland ever.

"I imagine my brothers are still as useless as ever. Padre ruled everything. Madre was his slave. The boys were his puppets."

"And that's why you left?" Storm said.

"Escaped," Henrietta said. "Thanks to Grandmadre in England."

Storm nodded. She understood all about escaping.

"That sounds like them now." Laura lowered herself into the chair next to Storm and rested a hand on her slightly rounded belly.

Storm heard the pounding of booted feet up the front steps. In seconds she'd see Blake.

The men came stomping in, as big and loud as she had anticipated, filling the ranch house until she thought it might burst its seams. At first, she didn't see Blake, and after a quick head count, she realized there were eight of them, not seven. Braydon pushed the extra man roughly inside. Storm saw Blake hang back, quiet but watchful.

"What's going on?" Laura asked.

"Found this guy snooping around out by your old camp, Henny. Claims he didn't know he was on Copper Moon land."

Storm recognized the newcomer as the reporter she'd seen hanging around at Braydon and Henrietta's wedding.

"Did you know he was going out there?" Braydon asked his wife.

"No," Henrietta said. "I was so busy with the wedding and all, I told him to go talk to Percy."

"Seems he didn't bother to talk to anyone, just made his way there of his own volition." Braydon nudged the man with the toe of his boot. "Isn't that right, buddy?"

"Buddy" was dusting the sleeve of his city coat as if he'd been soiled by his association with the Masons. "The name is Jones. John Jones. From the *Philadelphia Enquirer*."

"Well, John Jones, from the *Philadelphia Enquirer*, it's only a free country so long as you're not trespassing," Braydon said.

"I am truly sorry about that," Jones said. "I happened to see your neighbor riding in that direction, and my reporter instincts kicked in. There was something quite furtive in his actions."

"Which neighbor?" Brody asked sharply.

"Man by the name of Hawkes. Not a very pleasant fellow, I might add."

Storm could feel the air of tension permeate the room as soon as Jones spoke Hawkes's name.

"You followed Hawkes onto Copper Moon land?"

"Indeed."

"Did you see where we went?"

"I told you he was acting most secretive so I didn't get too close. Unfortunately, I lost him up near the ravine."

"What ravine?"

"You know, where those rock cliffs are. Looks like there might be an entrance to some caves farther along."

Storm saw the look Brody exchanged with Laura. Braydon and Henrietta had a similar exchange going on, which told her there was something significant about that particular section of the ranch. Something that the others weren't privy to.

"What happened next?" Brody said.

"I told you. Without knowing exactly which way he went, I didn't want to risk spooking him. I turned around, only this time I came across remnants of what looked like a dig site. I figured that's where Mr. Bloom and Miss Henrietta had been working."

Braydon's eyes narrowed. "What exactly are you doing a story on?"

Jones huffed with self-importance. "All anyone writes about these days is the gold rush. Folks are gold-rush crazy. I thought if I wrote about a different sort of treasure, riches that could be found almost anyplace, if one only knew where to look—"

"There's no pearl ship that we could find evidence of," Henrietta said.

"But there's other treasure waiting to be found," Jones said.

"Such as?" Henrietta said.

"Take, for instance, that gang of outlaws round these parts more'n twenty years ago robbing the stage coaches. Went by the name of Red's Rowdies. They made a big haul right before every last one of them disappeared from sight. No one's ever found where they stashed the goods." Jones paused to let his gaze touch each one of them in turn before he continued. "Lots of evidence leading to the fact that their loot is still around here. Maybe even buried on this ranch."

Storm noticed that Amanda, who normally had quite high color being a ginger, had turned unaccountably pale. She didn't miss the subtle way Bradley moved to her side, as if to protect her.

"That's a bunch of hogwash," Brody said. "My uncle worked this land all his life. He'd have known if there was anything like that buried around here."

"It's a big parcel," Jones said. "Pretty hard to monitor comings and goings from all quarters over the years."

"Are you done?" Brody crossed his arms over his chest in a way that implied their visitor was definitely finished.

"I'd like your permission to conduct further investigation of the property out near where I lost sight of Hawkes."

"Permission denied," Brody said. "Anything else?"

Jones looked deflated and determined by equal parts. "I'll be sticking around for a while, in case you change your mind."

"Don't count on it," Brody said as he moved to open the door in dismissal. "And Mr. Jones. We have a bit of a problem around here with wild animals attacking our herd from time to time. It would be a shame if you accidentally wandered onto the ranch and someone took a shot at you, thinking you were a coyote."

Jones plopped his hat back onto his head. "I'll take that under advisement." He reached the door, then turned to bow. "Ladies, the meal smells delicious. I didn't mean to keep you from your supper hour."

The air inside the ranch house grew quietly subdued. Storm sensed a lot of undercurrents had been stirred up by

Jones's visit. Undercurrents that had more impact on some family members than others.

"Are you sure I can't help?" Storm said, watching the ladies set the table while the gents disappeared outside, seeing to the horses and washing up.

Amanda waved her hand in what Storm assumed to be a negative response. "I'm so sorry that had to happen while you were here. I was looking forward to a nice quiet meal with no drama for Henrietta's last night."

Storm noticed Amanda's color return to normal as the conversation shifted to Henrietta's upcoming journey to visit her family in Argentina. Did everyone have secrets? Storm wondered. All this time she'd thought it was only her.

By the time the meal ended, it was as if Jones had never been there, stirring up any sort of discord or discomfort among the others. The conversation was lively, and although Storm contributed little she enjoyed being there, as well as observing the interaction between the others. The evening proved very different from what she recalled of family life in Ireland.

The only time she felt uncomfortable was when the conversation turned to ocean travel. "That must have been quite the crossing from Ireland to America," Amanda said. "Do you think you'll ever go back?"

"There's nothing and no one there for me to go back to," Storm said, uneasy at finding herself the topic of conversation.

Amanda leaned forward on her elbows. "What was New York like when you got there?'"

"Big. Crowded. Noisy. Dirty," Storm said. "Da tried to get work as a laborer, but everywhere he went, signs were posted saying 'Irish need not apply'."

"That's terrible," Laura said.

"I got work in a sewing factory," Storm said. "But Da died a broken man."

"Were you using those new-fangled sewing machines?"

"Tried to," Storm said. "The owner didn't cotton much to me. I never quite got the knack on account of I do better when I use my wrong hand. Scissors. Sewing machines. Even threading the needle." She swallowed thickly at the memory. "He wasn't a very nice man. Implied there were other things I could do better with my hands that didn't involve sewing." She pushed her plate away, no longer hungry.

"So that's when you came west?'

She nodded and stood. "I hope you don't think I'm rude, but it's late and I should be getting back to town."

Blake stood as well. "I'll see you back safe."

"Oh, no," she said. "You've already had a long day in the saddle, and—"

"And no Mason sends a lady out in the night on her own," Blake said.

"No point arguing," Amanda told her. "Next thing you know, they'll all escort you home."

"Now that would truly be unnecessary," Storm said. "Thank you, Blake."

When he reached out to help set her shawl around her shoulders, she found it cute that his movements were clumsy, as if he'd not done such a thing before.

The trip to town passed quickly, without much conversation between them, but she felt he might be letting down some of his previous guard toward her. She hoped, after they spent more time together while he installed the shelving in her wagon, that he might be comfortable enough so she could broach the topic of the various ways one could learn to read letters and eventually make sense of a few simple words.

The wagon stood right where she'd left it, but as they approached, Storm sensed something was wrong. The door gaped open, hanging askew on only one hinge. Blake saw it at the same time, and his hand went to his gun so fast she didn't have time to blink.

His arm shot out toward her and stopped her from going any closer. "Let me go first."

For once she had no argument, relieved to not be coming upon the destruction alone. For destruction was exactly what she faced. The ground near the wagon was littered with books or parts of books, pages ripped from their bindings. Even as she watched, the breeze caught loose pages and twirled them through the air.

There was no other sound, no other sign of movement besides the breeze. After scanning the area Blake spoke up. "It looks like whoever did this is long gone."

She and Blake dismounted at the same time.

Storm tried not to burst into tears as she picked her way over the ruined books and climbed into the wagon, where further destruction greeted her eye. The curtains had been ripped from the tiny window. Art work given her by happy children had been torn from the walls and ripped into pieces. Her one lone plant lay upside down in a pile of loose soil.

She let out a sob as she stooped down to rescue the one faded picture she had of her parents on their wedding day, ripped in half. Cushions lay scattered around, torn or upended. Shelves had been ripped from the walls. Books littered the floor nearly knee-high.

Before she knew it, Blake's arms were around her, hesitant at first, as if he was unused to offering comfort to another person. But as she sobbed against his shirtfront, dampening it with her tears, his touch grew more confident. He held her against him and stroked her hair, all the while making soothing noises as if she was a small child.

It had been so long since she had been held and comforted in any fashion, she forgot to be afraid. She hugged him back, absorbing his presence, his quiet strength, the warmth of his body against hers.

Eventually she stopped sniffling and stepped back. She pulled out a handkerchief and blew her nose in an unlady-like fashion that he didn't seem to notice, as he surveyed the damage.

"It's not as bad as it looks," he said finally. "Give me a few days and I'll have things put to rights like this never happened."

"Really?" She scrunched the hankie back into her bag. "You'd do that for me?"

He pushed her hair back from her face with a gentle hand. "I'm happy to do that for you, Storm. Now let's see what we can salvage from the mess outside. After that, I'll hitch up the horses, and we'll drive the wagon out to the ranch. No one would dare mess with it out there."

CHAPTER 3

There was absolutely nothing Storm hated on this earth more than being beholden to others. Back in Ireland, she had been old enough to know Da had been taken advantage of by the overseer of the estate where they lived.

What was intended to be an escape to a new life after ma died in childbirth, had been misery. Da was beholden first to the men who secured their passage, then to the sailors on the ship, abused by everyone as he tried to protect her.

At least, in America, she'd been able to take some of the burden from his shoulders when she first got work. There was no way of knowing, after he passed and she struck out for the promised land and a better life out west, that she'd wind up even more beholden to a man far more evil than the one in the garment factory.

This past year, as mistress of her own domain thanks to the book wagon, had truly been life-changing. No longer did she answer to anyone else. She made her own way, managing to bring joy into the lives of others at the same time.

In a matter of minutes, her life and everything that had been good about it, had been destroyed in a wanton frenzy of sheer malice. Worse yet, by a person or persons unknown.

"Do you think there is any chance it was just some rowdy kids blowing off steam?" she asked.

Blake had remained stone silent the entire time they worked to salvage what they could of the ruined books near the wagon and harness up the horses. Even now, as they drove back to the ranch, she couldn't begin to guess at his thoughts, for it was too dark to see his face. But she knew he was riled. She could tell by the way his shoulders were drawn up around his ears, and from how he continually scoured the pitch-black countryside, as if he expected fresh trouble at every bend in the road.

"Didn't appear to me like something kids would do," he said finally.

"Who would hate me that much? I haven't been here long enough to make any enemies. And there's nothing to be gained from such destruction."

Even in the dark, she sensed the way Blake's mouth drew tight.

"Some folks are just pure evil, through and through."

When they turned into the driveway of the Copper Moon, light spilled through the windows of the ranch house, a beacon welcoming them back. "Good. Everyone's still up. I want them to hear this."

Blake helped her down from the wooden seat. When she took a minute to find her footing in the dark, his hands reached for her, steadying her. She looked up, able to discern the shadowed hollows and planes of his face in the dim light behind them.

"You're being very kind to me," she said. Normally she didn't like being touched, but with Blake it felt different.

He ran an unsteady hand up her arm to her elbow. "I know what's it's like to be the outsider. To not have anyone. You're not alone, Storm. Not any more." He put a guiding hand against the small of her back. "Let's get you settled, then I'll see to the horses."

HAWKES LOOKED up to see the sheriff standing in his parlor as if he had every right to be there. Slowly and deliberately he set down his drink on the table next to him. "What are you doing here? It's late."

"Found something I believe belongs to you." Yates stepped to one side and revealed the two men who had been standing in the shadows behind him.

Hawkes stood up so fast he knocked over his glass of whiskey. "What the hell—"

"Caught 'em leaving a crime scene in town."

Hawkes walked right up to Denim and peered into his ugly mug. "What were you doing? And who the hell is that?"

"Haywire," Denim mumbled. "I tole you about him. You said it was okay to bring him on board."

Impatient, Hawkes turned back to the sheriff. "What were my men doing when you saw them?"

"Looked like they were making quite a mess of that book-lending wagon that's been around town the last little while."

Hawkes let loose with a string of expletives, pleased when he saw Denim and Haywire both flinch.

Denim attempted to square his shoulders. "I knew you didn't like it there, boss. Figured we'd teach that gal a lesson and get rid of her, out of your hair, so to speak."

"Do you have any idea what you've done?" Hawkes said, in deceptively mild tones.

"I thought—"

"You're too stupid to think," Hawkes roared. "We've been deliberately lying low. Waiting for the Masons to let down their guard. "Isn't that what we discussed?"

"This weren't nuthin' to do with them Masons," Denim said in surly tones.

"You dumbass. The woman was at that wedding. Of course she has something to do with the Masons."

Denim stared down at the floor in front of him. "I didn't know that."

"And there's a hell of a lot else you don't know. Just you be remembering that." He dismissed them with a wave of his hand. Once they were gone, he turned to Yates. "Appreciate you bringing them back, Sheriff. Can I get you a drink?"

"Don't mind if I do. Wish you'd hurry up and deal with those Masons. Don't like the way they act around me. As if I got no authority. What happened with the Mexicans and the copper?"

Hawkes had no intention of telling Yates how his business partners were getting cold feet. Give them time. They'd come crawling back. Just as soon as the Masons were out of his way once and for all and all his plans came to fruition.

THE MASONS WERE aghast when they heard what happened. Storm saw the way the brothers looked at each other, as if they were communicating something to each other with their eyes, rather than words.

"Do you have a suspicion who was responsible?" she asked.

"Got a few ideas," Brody said. "Don't worry. We'll look into it."

"What about the sheriff?" Storm asked. "Shouldn't he be informed?"

"Won't do you a lick of good," Blake said. "If it's who we think it was, the two of them are in cahoots."

"That's terrible!" Storm lowered herself shakily into an empty chair. Blake stood behind her, his hand resting on the back of the chair, as if prepared to come to her defense at a second's notice.

She took a quick look at the ladies to see if they noticed. Oh, they noticed all right. Laura even winked.

"We'll sort through things tomorrow," Amanda said. "Make a plan. For tonight, Blake did right to bring you here."

Henrietta spoke up. "Braydon and I are leaving early tomorrow. You'll stay in our cabin as long as you need to, until things get settled and your wagon is right as new."

"Oh, I can't possibly—"

"You can and you will," Henrietta said, in a tone that brooked no argument. Next to her, Braydon nodded as he gazed adoringly at his wife, as if unable to believe his good fortune. Storm felt a pang of envy for the happy couple.

"For tonight, you'll stay here in Brody's old room," Henrietta continued. "The sheets are clean. We're leaving early tomorrow. After you rise, you can move your things into our place. Blake will need room in the wagon to work. Isn't that right, Blake?"

"I can give you a hand," Benjamin said.

"We all will," said one of the twins.

"Good." Blake released his hold on her chair. "That's settled."

Laura rose. "I'll show you where you can wash up."

STORM FELT LESS than useless as Blake worked tirelessly on the interior of the wagon. She had little experience with ranch life. Amanda and Laura clearly had their own routine and she was reluctant to intrude into their marital ways. Mostly she stayed to herself in the cabin that had been built for Braydon and Henrietta, attempting to sort out loose pages and see if there was a way to repair some of the damage done to the books.

Blake walked in as she sat at the table, struggling with a pair of scissors, wielding them first in her right hand, then her left, then back to her right. Why was it so hard to straighten a ragged edge before she applied the hide glue?

After watching her for a long silent minute, he took the scissors from her hand and deftly finished what she started. She tried to make light of her clumsiness.

"You can see why I wasn't much use in the garment factory."

He continued to study the scissors as if he'd never seen a pair before. "Not your fault these don't work in your hand."

"Can't blame the scissors when it's operator clumsiness."

He smoothed his hand over hers. "You're not clumsy, Storm. Quit acting like you are. You're smart and beautiful and—" He removed his hand from hers, his face taking on a ruddy color with embarrassment, as if he wasn't accustomed to expressing himself in such terms.

Impulsively she caught his hand in both of hers. "Thank

you for your help. When this is over you have to let me do something for you."

He cleared his throat. "Came to fetch you so's you can see how the wagon's coming along."

BLAKE USHERED Storm over to the wagon, his heart pounding with sheer nerves. He hadn't meant to touch her the way he had, but seeing her struggle with those scissors had tugged at something deep inside, some part of him he didn't even know existed. Empathy. Understanding. A connection to another human being that he hadn't believed possible.

He started with the outside. "Benjamin came up with this idea, to make this wall here swing up and out of the way so folks can take a look at the books inside, not just wait for you to bring them out."

"Brilliant!" When she clapped her hands together in glee, he started to relax. He'd wanted everything perfect, but his work was only as good as the bones he started off with.

When he showed her inside, she gasped in what he hoped was a good way. Originally, things in the wagon had been pieced together in a haphazard fashion, shelves added as needed. The steps to the sleeping loft had been rickety as best. He had elected to strip the insides to the shell and start over again.

"It looks amazing!"

"Ben and Bradley helped when they had time."

She turned to him and threw her arms around him in a move that caught them both off guard. He took an unsteady step back, then a second. His hands automatically clasped around her trim waist to keep her steady. The wall with the ladder was at his back, Storm pressed up in front of him, showing no inclination to back away.

He could feel the soft swell of her bosom against his chest. He widened his stance for balance but she moved right into the V of his legs as if she was home, before she rested her head against his shoulder.

He didn't know what to do with his hands, so he let them follow his urges, trace the smooth line of her back from her hips to her shoulders before he slid down and cupped the rounded curve of her buttocks. She didn't move away but instead moved closer, her hips tilted against his male parts in a universal message.

Her face was toward his, lips parted slightly, begging for his kiss. His mouth found hers in a move that felt as natural as breathing, as if he had found home after a long, lonely journey. He felt her sigh into him, her sweet, warm breath filling his lungs and breathing for him, in case he forgot how.

He heard a faint mewling in the back of her throat as she wrapped her arms around his neck and pulled his head close, while her mouth moved beneath his, her tongue making tentative darting swipes until he realized he ought to open his lips.

Her tongue slid between his lips, tracing their shape, making tiny little nipping kisses before she tugged his lower lip inside of her mouth. He felt a rush of heated blood to his nether regions. His accelerated heartbeat pounded in his ears as he crushed her to him, flattening her chest against his, nudging her close enough to feel his male hardness.

They were interrupted by the jarring wrap of knuckles on the wall outside, seconds before the twins burst in.

❧

Storm stepped out of Blake's arms, breathing heavily. If the twins had any idea what they had just interrupted, they played dumb about it, each one talking over the other in an effort to be heard.

Storm willed her heart to slow to normal and her breath to return. She hadn't expected the way a quick thank you kiss to Blake quickly escalated to a fever pitch of passion she had never experienced. Especially not in the short time she'd been married.

"We had this idea. Saw it once in a rail car," one of the twins said.

"And we figured if it worked there, it should work here," his brother added.

"So we fiddled around with some iron pipe we had."

"And we think it turned out real good."

"If you like it."

"If you don't, you don't have to use it."

Storm glanced from one to the other in amusement. "Just what is this invention of yours?"

"Iron clips on the bookshelves. With matching clips on the ladder."

"That way the shelves can go all the way up to the roof of the wagon and you can still reach them."

"You can use the ladder that reaches up into your sleeping loft. Just move it around."

They both stopped, faces alight with a hopeful expectation.

Storm turned to Blake. "I think it sounds brilliant. What do you think?"

"Sure does. I only wish I'd thought of it," Blake said, ruefully.

"No worries, man. That's what family is for. Help each other out."

"Thank you very much." Storm looked closely at each twin as she spoke, determined to tell them apart. "Bishop." She shook the hand of the one closest to her. "Barron." She took the second one's hand.

"Welcome, ma'am," they said, in unison. But she could tell she had got their names right, and they were pleased by that.

"Looks like you two won't be playing any switch-up games with Storm. She's got you figured," Blake said.

"Must be all them books you have, ma'am," Bishop said.

"You're welcome to borrow any books you'd like. Anytime you want."

Barron picked out a volume on magic. "This one looks interesting. Doesn't it, Bishop?"

"Sure does."

"What's it about?" She could tell that Blake hated that he had to ask.

"Magic," she said. "Illusions and escapology."

"Don't let them read that," Blake said. He sounded serious. "They get up to enough mischief pulling one over on folks, without the help of some new tricks learned from a book."

"We need this," Bishop said seriously. "We're working on a plan for putting one over on Hawkes when the time is right."

"That's right." Barron nodded seriously.

"Does Brody know about this?" Blake asked.

"Not yet," Bishop said. "But he will."

"Right now, we'll show you how these ladder hooks are going to work."

⁓

UNDER BLAKE'S GUIDANCE, the book wagon became far more functional than anything Storm could have imagined. The ladder hooks from the twins were sheer genius. Benjamin had shown up at the cabin several times to help with the repair of any salvageable volumes, and proved himself very adapt at the task.

"You look like you've done this before," Storm said.

"Spent some time as a book-binder when I was in prison."

"You were in prison?" she asked. "Whatever for?"

"Killed a man. Shot him dead for trying to rape my mother." He looked over at her with a shrug. "I wasn't locked up long, once they found out how young I was. But by the time they let me go, my ma had married and moved on."

"She left you?" Storm was aghast.

"Reckon she never wanted me in the first place," Benjamin said. "It's a hard life for a woman alone on the prairie. Can't say I blame her much."

"But that's— that's—" Storm caught herself. Reminded herself not to judge others until she'd walked in their shoes. She wasn't all that different from Benjamin and his mother.

"Well your skill is certainly appreciated," she said.

"Happy to help out. We all do what we can around here."

"How did you come to meet Brody and the others?"

"It was in the gambling hall. I didn't have much to lose, was bluffing my way through, pissing off some of the other players. Things were starting to get pretty heated when Brody joined the game. He cleaned us all out and deflected everyone's anger from me."

"He must be a very good card player, if he could do that."

"I hear he takes after his old man in that regard. Anyway, I saw one of the fellows follow him out. Stopped him from doing Brody harm. Brody liked the way I handled a gun. Said there was a place for me here if I was of a mind." He glanced around. "Figured I'd try it for a while. Once I settled in, I never saw any reason to leave. Besides, we got some unfinished business with one of the neighbors."

He stood before she could question him further. "Reckon you could stick around too, if you were of a mind. The ladies like you."

"Oh, well, I just ..." Storm didn't know what to say. Somehow she doubted Blake would share Benjamin's enthusiasm at her continued presence.

"I'm really just here while the wagon gets outfitted. Then I've got my work to get back to."

"Understand."

Storm watched him leave, wondering how she'd feel if the same casual offer to stay had been made by Blake. Before she reminded herself of the one obvious reason she couldn't stay, even if she wanted to.

"NEED some help putting these books back, Storm?" Blake asked, once the shelves had been installed and painted to his satisfaction.

"Yes please," she said. "You can reach the tall shelves and I won't have to move the ladder. Not that it isn't a godsend," she added.

"Where do you want me to start?"

"If I sort them into categories and you file them alpha-betically, by the author's name, that would be a great help," she said. Too late she realized what she just said. The look on Blake's face spoke volumes.

"Don't reckon I'd be much help after all," he said, hands

stuffed into his pockets, as if he couldn't bear to even touch the books after what she had just said.

"You know what?" she said brightly. "Forget the author's names. Let's shelve them according to color. That'll work really well and look nicer, too."

She watched as Blake's shoulders slowly relaxed. Once the books were shelved, she could sort them alphabetically after she left the ranch. If Blake ever noticed, which he probably wouldn't, she could just blame the patrons for mixing things up.

Blake had been such a help to her, it was time she did what she could to help him.

"Do you mind walking me back?" she asked that evening, after the supper had been consumed and cleaned up at what she had come to think of as the "big house". The cabin she was staying in was cute and cozy and smelled like fresh-cut wood, but there was no denying the comfortable sense of history and belonging the old ranch house exuded. She figured if those walls could talk, they would have quite a story to tell.

Storm felt unaccountably nervous as she and Blake strolled the short distance from the ranch house to Henrietta and Braydon's cabin. She paused when they reached the front door and faced Blake, praying for the right words to make her offer without insulting him. The moon was big and bright in the sky, making the yard nearly as well lit as during the day, only more silver. Blake didn't seem in any big hurry to say good night. He removed his hat and turned it around and around, as if needing something to keep his hands busy.

She took a breath and placed one hand lightly on his forearm. She felt his muscles tense but he didn't pull away. "You've done so much for me lately," she said.

"It was nothing," Blake said.

"It was a lot more than nothing," Storm said, her words tumbling over themselves in her eagerness to have her say before she chickened out and changed her mind. "And I, in turn, would appreciate it if you let me do something for you."

"Shucks, Storm, I don't need nothing. I makes me feel good knowing I was able to help. That you'll be safe in your travels." He tilted his head to one side in a way she found endearing. "I'm kinda hoping you'll look in back here next time you're in Bullet."

"You know I will," she said. "There's lots to plan with Amanda, about her town hall project. To say nothing of Laura having her baby. I have the feeling the ranch is going to be the place to be."

He blew out a breath. "I have to say, it feels a whole lot better with you here."

"You're very lucky to have what you and the others have created here," she said. "Wait. Don't say anything. Just hear me out." She paused and shifted her weight from foot to foot. "I've seen the way you've looked at the books."

"Just books," Blake mumbled.

"I can tell the letters don't make a whole lot of sense to you the way they do to most other folks."

She saw him stiffen, felt him fighting the urge to bolt.

"You're not the only one who has that difficulty, Blake. I've helped others. And I would be really happy if you would let me at least try to help you."

She could see the war of expressions crossing his face in the moonlight. The initial urge to deny what she was saying, followed by the wash of shame.

"It's nothing to be ashamed of, Blake. Plenty of folks are

just too lazy to read. I can tell, with you, it's something different."

He looked down at the ground beneath his feet. "It's no use. Brody tried his best to teach me when I first came here to live. I'm just hopeless. Too stupid to learn. That's what they told me at the orphanage."

"They're wrong," Storm said. "You just need a different way of learning from most folks, is all."

"Doesn't matter," he said. "I get along just fine."

He plopped his hat on his head as if preparing to take his leave. Storm took a breath and launched herself at him. His arms closed round her, so good and big and strong. She choked back the sudden urge to stay there forever. "Please, Blake. Please let me help you." Her words came out in a near sob of shame. "I've done some bad things in my life. I've been trying ever since to make amends by doing good."

CHAPTER 4

Blake really wished he hadn't agreed to have Storm try to help him with his letters. He'd gotten by just fine for this long without reading and writing. What if she tried her best and he still couldn't grasp the concept? They'd both feel bad. She'd wind up going out of her way to avoid him because of the awkwardness.

The prospect made his gut churn, as if he'd eaten something that didn't agree with him. He didn't want to lose Storm's friendship. Before Brody started wooing Laura, and the brothers had all got in the act in an effort to teach Brody to smarten up, he hadn't realized it was even possible to be friends with a woman. He'd discovered it was nice. Women had a soft kindness to them that made his soul ache.

He sighed. He also knew better than get used to Storm, to her being around. Soon enough she'd hitch up that book wagon of hers and go back to what she'd been doing before Braydon and Henrietta's wedding. Sure, she might talk about coming back to help Amanda get things set up, but it would be a fleeting visit at best.

He wondered for the umpteenth time what the bad

things were that Storm claimed she had done. He couldn't imagine a sweet, itty-bitty thing like her doing anything bad. Sounded like her life had been hard and lonely, same as his. That's what this was all about. No other reason he felt the way he did, like he'd known her forever instead of just a short time.

She'd been so distraught the other night, he'd promised he'd let her try to help him with the learning, even though the very idea stabbed dread into his heart. The past rose up to choke him. The teachers. The other kids. Taunting him. Calling him a dummy.

He'd wanted to die that day he met Brody. Had egged those bullies on, hoping they would do what he hadn't the courage for. To end his miserable life. Instead, he'd wound up here, the first one in Brody's new family. And now some little gal waited for him on the other side of the door, counting on him learning something he knew to be impossible. Something she felt duty-bound to try.

He hadn't even knocked before the door flew open. "I was afraid you might change your mind," Storm said.

"I said I'd be here," he said gruffly. "Not happy about it but figure the sooner you realize I'm hopeless, the sooner we both can get back to what we were doing before this all happened."

Storm gazed up at him with those big, unusual-colored eyes of hers. Sometimes he thought they were brown. Other times he could swear they were green.

"It's strange," she said, tilting her head as if she was trying to see him in a different light. As if she felt as conflicted as he did. "For the first time ever, I'm not looking forward to hitting the road and moving from town to town. And that's your fault, Blake Mason."

He blanched. "My fault?"

She dimpled prettily, peeking up at him from beneath lowered lashes. "You and your entire Mason clan. You're a pretty irresistible group to find myself part of. Even for a short while."

Blake didn't know what to say. Women might have a kind softness. They also had a different way of expressing themselves than menfolk did. Never much of a speaker, he was all twisted in knots and tongue-tied. When he looked back at her, he realized she was gesturing him to come inside.

He stopped short just inside the parlor. The room was littered with pictures. Chunks of paper. Pencils. "What's all this?"

"Just some things we're going to try. We'll start with a few simple words and letters, and a way for you to remember them."

A wave of nausea swept over him.

He never should have come!

The fact that he'd wanted to see Storm, to spend time with her, wasn't reason enough to put himself through this kind of torture.

Blake planted his feet apart and crossed his arms over his chest. His gaze slid toward the door. Toward escape.

As if she sensed his urge to bolt, Storm tugged on his arm, pulled him over to the settee, and lowered herself next to him. "There are a lot of letters that look really similar and they can be hard to tell apart. Sometimes pictures help. The other day you told me, when you're fixing to build something, you take a picture of the space with your mind. Then when you're building it, you know where it's going and where the different parts should be. Remembering words and letters is much the same."

Damn, she smelled good. He wanted to lean in and

nuzzle the soft-looking skin on her neck, to take a deep sniff and drown in her female softness.

She leaned toward him, her shoulder brushing his as she pulled a piece of paper toward her and wrote some letters. Looked to him like a stick, two circles in the middle, and a funny letter on the end that looked backwards or upside down.

"This word is 'look'. And here is the way you can remember." To his amazement, she drew an eyeball in the middle of each circle.

"What do you do with your eyes?" she asked.

"You look," Blake said, his tone tinged in wonder. "But how am I going to remember that when there are no eyeballs?"

"You're going to look at it a lot. Take a picture of it with your mind. I'll put it on a card with the picture on one side and the plain word on the back. One day, when you look at the plain word, you'll remember the missing eyeballs, and be able to read it." She gave him an encouraging smile.

"This one here on the end." He pointed. "It looks like it's pointing the wrong way."

"That's the letter 'k'. And it's a confusing one, because it makes the sound 'kuh'. But there's a different letter, looks an awful lot like the 'o' here in the middle." She pointed to the eyeball letter. "Except it has an opening on one side that makes the same sound."

"That's stupid," Blake said.

"I agree." She smiled up at him in a way that had his heart doing flip-flops. "I hope you don't mind, but I helped myself to some sand from that pile near the barn. Cut some papers into a few shapes of the difficult letters, like 'k' and glued sand on the top with that hide glue you got me for fixing the books. That way you can feel it, commit the feeling to memory, and you'll never forget which way the legs of the letter point."

From a notebook, she pulled out a large sand-covered letter and placed it on the table between them. Then she picked up his hand and guided it on the sandy letter. With her fingers atop his, she urged him to trace the shape.

Damn, she made it difficult to concentrate. The rough texture of the sandy shape beneath his fingers was in direct contrast to the softness of her fingertips against the top of his hand. How the hell was he supposed to think about the name and shape of the letter when all he wanted to do was to crush her mouth beneath his and topple her over on the settee and—

Friends, he reminded himself.

In his world, you didn't go around kissing your friends, let alone think about all the other things you had the urge to do with them.

"You're right." His voice sounded as scratchy as the letter beneath his fingers. "Feeling the sand on the shape makes it easier to remember."

"We're not going to do too much for one day. I'm just going to make you a few cards with pictures so you know what each word means. You can take the cards with you and look at them whenever you have a few minutes to spare. Just casual-like. Don't try too hard. Just think about the picture you like to take in your mind before you start to build something. It'll start to feel natural after a while as long as you don't push it."

When she started to lift her hand from atop his, he caught it with his other hand and urged it back down onto his. He tried his best to sound sincere, his eyes on hers signaling a hope he hadn't felt in a long time. "I think I do a lot better learning when you're helping me like this." He flipped his hand over and linked her fingers through his.

Was that sadness he saw in her eyes? "I won't always be here, Blake."

He bit back the urge to tell her he wanted her to always be here. How somehow, her presence made him feel better. Stronger. More capable. More the man he wanted to be.

But he couldn't say that. It would make him sound weak. He abhorred weakness.

"'Course not," he said gruffly.

STORM KNEW she ought to go. She had already overstayed her welcome here at the Copper Moon. Not that anyone was sending her hints to that end or anything. On the contrary, she had fallen into a comfortable routine. When the men were out working, she spent time with Laura and Amanda, who were knitting and sewing tiny items for a layette for Laura and Brody's expected new arrival.

But mostly she looked forward to the evenings and the time she spent with Blake, who proved an adept pupil and could now print his own name, as well as read a few simple words.

"I don't know when your baby is going to wear all these clothes," Storm said, watching as the pile of tiny, knitted garments grew on a daily basis.

The two women exchanged a look. Amanda blushed. "You're the first one to find out. Other than Laura. And Bradley, of course. But Laura's little one will have a wee friend before long."

"Oh. Well then. We'd best get cracking." Delighted to be taken into their confidence, Storm returned to her sewing.

Blake had fashioned a cradle for the baby, and she had been busy sewing blankets from a soft, wool yard good, edged with some satin ribbon she purchased in Yuma.

"You're a really fast sewer," Laura said admiringly, watching Storm manipulate the old clunky sewing machine she barely ever used.

"Not really," Storm said. "I wish the machine was built the other way around so I could face it over here." She held up her left hand. "I do things better with this hand, but given the way the machine is, I'm forced to use the other one."

"I see what you mean," Amanda said, watching as Storm struggled with a pair of scissors. "Maybe I should teach you to play the piano."

Storm looked at her. "Why on earth would I want to play the piano?"

"Because each hand has a role in the music. It just might even things out for you."

"There's no point," Storm said brusquely. "I'm leaving soon and won't have any chance to practice."

"Maybe sometime in the future," Amanda said, unperturbed by Storm's shortness. "Once the music hall is built, I plan to offer lessons to anyone who wants to learn."

"Are the plans finished being drawn?"

Amanda nodded, her voice bubbly with enthusiasm. "I hired a work crew from Yuma. They should be ready to start in a few weeks."

"You hired them?" Storm said. "And they're prepared to be working for a woman?"

"Not exactly," she said. "They think Bradley is their boss."

"You're lucky," Storm said with a sigh. "To have a husband who loves you and supports you."

"He does love me," Amanda said, her skin pinkening. "He worries I've taken on too much with the music hall project, yet he was the one who gave me the idea in the first place."

Laura looked up from her knitting. "Who will help Blake with his letters, once you leave?"

"I'll be back at some point," Storm said. "Besides, I can't stay here living in Braydon and Henrietta's cabin."

"I know!" Amanda clapped her hands together. "Percy's leaving. You can move into my house in town where I used to live."

"Oh, no, I—"

"Please," Amanda said. "I don't want it left empty. It's the perfect idea. That way you have a home base, a place to come back to."

Storm looked at the excited, hopeful faces of her new friends. "I'll think about it," she said. The thought of having a place to call her own was tempting and scary at the same time. As was the thought that she could continue to see Blake from time to time. Maybe she really could have a future, in spite of everything in her past.

No, she told herself, sadly. Keeping on the move was for the best. The easiest way not to get found.

HAWKES FACED Denim across the dusty surface of his desk. None of his household staff was allowed in here. He didn't trust them not to snoop into things that were none of their concern.

Denim was a con, just recently out of jail, and not very bright, which he had certainly proved the other night when he and his idiot friend roughed up the book wagon. As far as Hawkes was concerned, Denim being mostly a half-wit made him perfect for this latest job. He'd do what he was told without asking nosy questions.

"So this reporter?" Denim said, one booted foot resting on his opposite knee. His burly frame dwarfed the leather chair in Hawkes's office, and he picked his teeth as he spoke. "You sure you don't want me to take care of him?"

"Just keep an eye on him. Let me know where he goes and who he talks to. And be sure and let me know if he gets too close to that one area I told you about."

"What's so special about that place, anyway?"

Hawkes glared at him. "Remember how you stayed alive in jail? Keep your eyes open and your mouth shut. Got it?"

Denim pushed off, and ambled to his feet. "You're the boss."

"Something you would do well to remember."

"What do you want me to do if he does get too close to that spot? Want me to take care of him?"

"No. I want you to run into him all friendly like. Then I want you to deliver him back here to me."

Denim frowned. "Why do you get all the fun?"

"Same reason you got locked up for a long time and I didn't. I'm smarter."

BLAKE PULLED the rig to a stop in front of Amanda's house in town, where Percy had been staying with Henrietta before the wedding. Now that the treasure-hunt had been officially called off, Percy had reached out to the brothers for a lift to the train station in Yuma.

Blake wasn't sure why he got volunteered for the job. What could he possibly have to say to someone whose entire life revolved around book learning, then teaching those learnings to others in some fancy school back in England?

Percy must have been watching for him. "I say, Blake. Can I get a hand with the bags?"

"Oh. 'Course." Blake shook off his thoughts and galloped up the steps to wrestle the awkward steamer trunk down to the street and into the wagon. Percy followed with several smaller valises.

"I really appreciate the lift," Percy said. "Much nicer than being sandwiched into the stagecoach with folks not over-much acquainted with soap and water."

"Guess you're looking forward to the next great adventure," Blake said. "Where is the best spot you've ever visited?"

"Hmmmm." Percy narrowed his eyes as if deep in thought.

Blake expected his companion's response to be Greece or Egypt or some other exotic place that hadn't existed in his vocabulary before Percy and Henrietta came to town.

"This will likely surprise you, but I think my favorite place so far has been Bullet."

Blake narrowly avoided steering the horses off the road, he was so shocked by the other man's answer. "Bullet?" he repeated, unable to completely trust his hearing. "But you've been everywhere!"

"Not quite," Percy said modestly. "I'll admit, it surprises me too. But there's something about this place. Kind of raw and wild, yet warm and welcoming at the same time. That last part, of course, is all due to your family."

"I'll be." If Blake was stumped for conversation before, he was doubly stumped now.

"A lot of people think they're missing out because they haven't been all over," Percy said. "But at the end of the day, all humans really need is comfort and companionship. Do you know why people are emigrating from Europe to the colonies?"

Blake shook his head.

"It's because their life where they were living wasn't comfortable. They're looking to create a better life for themselves and their families. Either that, or they have no family. No reason to stick around. And they're hoping to find that special something that was missing, over here in the new world."

"Like Storm and her da."

"Exactly like Storm and her da. Starting a new life can be difficult. But it can also be very rewarding. You're one of the lucky ones, Blake. You've got everything right here. No need to go gallivanting. Of course," he continued, "some folks don't care to settle down. Always on the hunt for something better than what they have." He turned in his seat and looked Blake straight in the eye. "I'll let you in on a little secret. There is seldom anything better than what a body has, right here, right now."

Blake digested Percy words. Finally, he raised an issue close to his heart.

"Miss Storm," he said. "You think she's one of those folks that's always on the hunt for something new? I mean, she drives that book wagon all over."

"I don't think that about Storm at all. It strikes me that she well may be looking for an excuse to stay put for a change. A reason not to leave. Henrietta was much the same. She fought it hard, but turned out her heart was wherever Braydon was. Something in him nourishes that empty spot inside her."

Was that how he felt? Blake wondered. Did Storm somehow feed an inner emptiness?

"It's scary," he blurted out. "Caring that much for another person."

"I think it boils down to one word. Protection," Percy said.

"Protection?"

"Who is it more important you protect? Yourself? Or the ones you care about?"

"The others, of course," Blake said without hesitation.

"Exactly. And once a person gets that figured out, the way you and your brothers have, everything else just seems to fall into place. At least, for the lucky ones." He gave Blake another knowing look. "Don't miss out on being one of the lucky ones, Blake."

HEAVY-HEARTED, Storm tucked the last of her belongings into the drawers in the back of the book wagon. She'd already stayed here at the Copper Moon longer than she should have. Far longer than was smart.

She looked around, part of her already missing the ranch and the folks who lived here. Strangers who had opened their home and their hearts to her.

"Hey, Storm."

Oh, dear. Blake.

The one person it would be hardest to say goodbye to.

"I just got back from driving Percy to the train station in Yuma. You fixing to move to Amanda's house now that he's gone?"

"I can't," she said sadly. "I have to get going." She took a shaky breath. She hadn't thought it would be this hard, saying goodbye. But then she'd never said goodbye before, at least not to anyone she cared about.

"But ... I thought ... Aren't you helping Amanda get things set up with a library and all?"

Suddenly Storm felt inexplicably weary. "I'm not sure I'll be able to do that."

His handsome face puckered in confusion. "Did I do something wrong?"

"Of course not!"

Trust Blake to blame himself.

"Then why are you leaving and not coming back?"

"It's complicated, Blake."

He stared her down, unblinking. "You said you did bad things. I don't care what you've done in the past. I know good people sometimes have to do bad things. It doesn't make them a bad person."

"You just keep thinking that. No matter what you might hear." Her eyes began to well up and she blinked rapidly to clear her vision.

Blake pressed his lips together as if conflicted. "I made something for you. I was going to wait to give it to you as a thank-you for helping me with my letters."

"I wasn't much help," she said.

"Of course you were. You made me realize anything is possible. That I'm not the dummy everyone used to tell me I was. That I just learn things different, is all."

She clenched her fists. Implored the heavens to not let her cry. At least not in front of him. "And don't you go forgetting that. I think Laura will be able to help you with your word learning. I showed her some of the things we were doing."

"Pretty soon Laura's going to be busy with her young 'un.

Anyway." He pulled his hand out from behind his back. "I wanted to give this to you to take with you."

"Scissors?" she said puzzled.

"I made them special. So you can use your other hand in them." He demonstrated, snipping the air between them, before he tucked the fingers of her left hand into the holes. The metal of the scissors was warm from his hand.

"Oh, my word," she said. "They feel so good."

"Made 'em smaller on account of you have such little hands," he said.

"They're perfect. How did you know?"

"When we were touching the sand letters. I was taking a picture in my head of your hand on top of mine. That way I knew how to make them the right size for you."

Storm swallowed past the suddenly huge lump in her throat. "No one has ever, in my entire life, done anything so nice for me."

He looked at her and nodded. "Funny. I feel the same way about you and the letter learning."

Once again, her eyes threatened to fill with tears. There was a painful weight on her chest. Her lungs felt constricted, as if she couldn't quite draw a deep enough breath.

"You okay?" He was watching her with concern.

She gave her head a shake to clear her thoughts and her vision. "Never better."

"Good. Then I got something that needs said before you go. Stay here, Storm. Marry me and be my wife."

Dizzily, she swayed toward him, afraid she might faint.

He caught her and held her. Safe. If only she could stay and feel safe forever.

"I can't." Her words came out in the barest of whispers. "I'm already married."

CHAPTER 5

Blake looked down at the woman in his arms, barely able to register the words he had just heard her say. "My hearing must be off. It sounded an awful lot like you said you were already married."

"It's true," she said sadly. "After Da died, I saw an ad in the newspaper. A rancher out west was looking for a bride. I answered him and he sent me the money for the train."

"You married someone you never even met." Blake still held her, but she felt different in his arms. Like he was holding onto a stranger.

"I wanted a better life than the one I had in New York," she said. "Turned out he was meaner than a snake. I wasn't there long before he came at me one day in the barn. Told me I did a bad job of mucking out the stalls and that he had to teach me a lesson. Had a whip in his hand and a crazy look in his eye."

Blake saw red. He'd been bullied his entire youth, but for a man to treat a beautiful woman like Storm that way—a woman he was lucky enough to be married to? A woman who deserved his protection, not his abuse?

Blake rubbed Storm's back as he felt the Storm he knew slowly coming back to him. He kept his feelings to himself. The anger and the fury. The urge to teach the bully a lesson about picking on someone unable to defend themselves.

"He'd had a wife before me. She hung herself from the rafters in the barn rather than stay married to him. Because of that, he never let me out of his sight. I was little more than his prisoner."

Blake let out a low whistle between his teeth, feeling the terror Storm must have endured at the hands of the man she'd been married to.

"When he came at me with the whip, I knew he wouldn't kill me, but that he'd hurt me bad. So bad I'd never be able to get away." She drew a shaky breath. "There was a pitch fork I'd been using in the stall. I grabbed it as he came toward me. He knocked it from my hand, then he tripped and fell on it. He wasn't dead but there was blood. So much blood. I knew he'd fix the law on me, so I just grabbed what I could and ran. Ran as hard and as fast as I could to get out of town and far away."

She paused and pushed a shaky hand through her hair. Blake doubted she realized she was still in his arms. "I don't know how long I was on the run for. I ran at night and hid during the day."

"But you made it. You got away." Pride for her strength and determination rang through his voice.

"One day I was too tired and hungry to run any more. That's when the book wagon came by. Miss Millie was her name. Said I could ride with her and help out. Never told me she was dying till the end." Her voice had a far-away tone, telling him she was lost in her memories. "No one at her burial but me. Sad, really. All those people that she helped by bringing them books. I kept the wagon going. No one in any of the towns I went to even asked after her." Storm shrugged. "Maybe they were just used to folks up and dying."

Blake thought of the night he'd met Brody. When all he'd wanted was to die. No one would have mourned him or missed him either.

His arms tightened around Storm. "I guess the important thing is that she died doing what she wanted to do."

"Truly. Anyway, that's why I have to go. And that's why I can't marry you."

Blake had a thought. "Where was this, that you lived when you were married?"

"Just outside of Colorado Springs. Why?"

"No reason." Blake released her abruptly. "Just thought of something I need to do."

As soon as Blake left, Storm said her goodbyes to Laura and Amanda, suitably vague as to when she'd be back this way again. "Say goodbye to the brothers for me. And give Henrietta and Braydon my regards when they get back from Argentina."

She saw the look Amanda and Laura exchanged.

"We'll say your farewells to the others for you," Laura said. "But what about Blake?"

"Already said goodbye to him." And just like that, he'd lit off. Didn't appear as he'd miss her as much as she'd miss him.

"Just goodbye?" Laura asked, in such a way Storm wondered if she knew that Blake had asked her to marry him and stay on.

"That's right," Storm said. "I told him you'd help him some with his letter learning."

"What about the music hall?" Amanda asked. "The first of the building materials has already been delivered. Once the crew gets started, it shouldn't take long at all. You promised you'd help me get the library set up."

"I didn't promise," Storm reminded her. "I said I'd help out if I was here. You've already got the ideas. You'll do fine. If I'm ever back this way, I'll bring you some books for it," Storm added, aware it was not at all what her friend was hoping to hear, pushing down the feeling that she was letting other folks down. She needed to be thinking of herself. "I really have to get going."

After a few more tearful hugs and vague promises to return one day, she hitched up the horses and slowly made her way toward town. The horses' pace quickened as they passed Hawkes's place. As if they sensed something bad in the air. Something evil.

AFTER STORM'S DISCLOSURE, Blake rode like the wind into Yuma, where he raced into the train station and bought a ticket. He barely made it on board as the train started to pull out of the depot. He found Percy in the second car.

"Blake?" Percy put down his reading when Blake took the seat opposite, staring at him as if he couldn't quite believe what he was seeing.

"Got a situation," Blake said. "One I need your help with."

BEFORE SHE LEFT Bullet for good, Storm couldn't resist one last look at the site where the music hall would soon be built. As Amanda had said, lumber and other building supplies had been delivered, stacked up on one side of the land. She stopped the wagon across the street from the site and tried to envision the finished structure. Two stories high as laid out on the drawings. Alive with folks coming and going, everyone making the most of the new addition to their town.

Just then, at the far end of the road, she saw three rough-looking men cross the street furtively, looking over their shoulders as they made their way onto the building site. She shrank back, hoping they didn't see her sitting in the wagon. Minutes later, the slight breeze brought the unmistakable smell of kerosene her way, followed by the crackle of fire and smell of smoke. Seconds later she saw flames licking through the pile of lumber.

Storm turned the wagon around and raced back to the Copper Moon as fast as she could urge the horses to go. Amanda appeared in the doorway of the ranch house.

"Forget something?"

The words tumbled over themselves in Storm's haste to get them out. "Something terrible. There's a fire in town. All your lumber and materials are ablaze."

Laura joined them, a rifle in her hand. As soon as Storm stopped talking, Laura raised the gun and fired a shot in the air, closely followed by a second. "The men will know there's an emergency but no danger to us."

After that, things happened in a blur. The menfolk arrived from various corners of the ranch, and Brody organized them into a team to head to town. "You'll need the fire buckets," Laura said.

"Probably too late for that," Bradley said, with a sad look directed to his wife.

"Take them in case," Laura said.

Amanda climbed up into the wagon with Storm. "We'll follow."

Storm could tell Brody was keen to join the others but reluctant to leave his pregnant wife behind. "Do you feel like coming with us, Laura?" she asked.

"Try to stop me," Laura said as she hitched up her skirt and climbed into the front of the wagon. "I'm having a baby, not dying of a contagious disease." She shot Amanda a telling look. "Isn't that right, my friend?"

By the time they reached town, a brigade of townsfolk were busy dumping buckets of water on the few spots still smoldering. A circle of onlookers milled about. The Masons took over the bucket brigade while Bradley stopped to thank everyone who helped out. Storm and the ladies stood off to one side.

"It's hotter than a firecracker out," one of the locals said. "But I've never known the sun to spark a fire on a pile of lumber."

"Not without some help," one of the others added.

"Sure glad it didn't spread," said a third. "Lucky the materials were on the far side away from the fence."

Storm noticed no one mentioned the smell of kerosene. It must have burned off.

"Did anyone see anything?" Brody asked.

Storm remained silent. She'd been the only one around at the time the fire started, other than the arsonists themselves.

Not until the fire was well and truly out did the Mason brothers put down their buckets. The crowd of onlookers had dwindled to a small handful.

Storm wandered close enough to overhear Benjamin talking to Brody. "Is there any way Hawkes could have found out Bradley and Amanda bought this land?"

"They were careful to put it in a company name rather than their own," Brody said. "But someone could have got to the lawyer."

The twins arrived from the fire site, sweaty and sooty. "Looks like a fair amount of damage," Barron said.

"But some stuff can be salvaged for sure."

Bradley joined the men. "We are lucky it was broad daylight out. The locals acted fast to stop the blaze. Be a different story if this had been at night. By the time anyone realized what was happening it would have been too late."

Amanda joined the men and hooked her arm through Bradley's. "Need I remind you who didn't want me to buy insurance on the project?"

Bradley made a face. "Yes, dear. That was most forward-thinking of you."

"I was also thinking of my investor," Amanda said.

Storm recalled a conversation about a mysterious investor that Amanda and Laura referred to as an "angel investor". She wondered who the mystery person was, and felt relieved to learn that even though there had been significant loss, it wasn't enough to derail her friend's project.

Since she still had Laura and Amanda with her, Storm had no choice but to turn the wagon back in the direction of Copper Moon.

"I guess Blake stayed behind to keep an eye on things at the ranch?" she asked. She'd noticed his absence right off but hadn't wanted to say anything.

"Blake? No," Amanda said. "He lit out of here earlier like a crazy man. Said he had things to see to." She slanted a sideways look at Storm. "Thought you might know where he went."

BLAKE LEANED FORWARD in his seat across from Percy, legs apart, forearms resting on his knees. He'd never been on a train before. He'd also never asked anyone for help before. Early survival had taught him it was better not to let on a body needed anything from anyone. Need would be taken as a sign of weakness and used against him.

Even on the ranch, he didn't feel quite part of the camaraderie shared by the others. He could pull his weight no matter what, farming or ranching or driving cattle. But he preferred being alone in the barn, working on projects designed to make everyone's lives easier, than out on the trail with the others. He didn't have Brody's quiet strength, Braydon's way with folk, Bradley's gift with animals, the twins' quick reflexes and savvy, or Benjamin's skill with guns.

He'd kept his distance from Percy also, during the man's time in Bullet, more than a little intimidated by anyone's years of book learning at university. He'd heard Henrietta talk about Oxford. How they let women attend classes but not write exams, so they couldn't get degrees like the men. How she'd hoped to see that all change. Such talk was too much for Blake to even grasp so he didn't try.

Percy didn't quiz him about why he was there but gave him time to gather his thoughts.

"I hope I didn't say something earlier, on the drive here, that created this urgent situation?"

"Everything you said was right," Blake said. "Stuff I needed to hear."

"Not necessarily," Percy said. "One should always take the words of others with a handful of salt."

"Salt?" Blake puzzled.

"Never mind," Percy said. "What, pray, prompted what I can only consider rather uncharacteristic actions on your part?"

"You said you're headed for Colorado."

"That's right. I hear Colorado Springs is a bit of Olde England, with a marvelous spa. Where are you off to?"

"Same place," Blake said. "Need to check on a rancher who lives near there. Fellow who got himself stabbed with a pitchfork. Find out if he's alive or dead. If they ever caught the person who did it." He glanced at Percy. "Not sure of his name, though. That's where you come in. I was hoping you could maybe ask to see some old newspapers or something once we get there. Happened a year or so back."

Percy cleared his throat. "I assume you have more than a passing interest in this story."

"Could say."

"And that I'm to be discreet with any inquiries?"

"Figure you'd be good at that. What with all your treasure-hunting experience and schooling and all. I can pay you some. Not much."

"Not necessary." Percy picked up his newspaper. "Happy to help out a friend."

Blake sat back, watching Percy as he resumed his reading. Had the other man just referred to Blake as a friend?

He'd never considered himself a friend to the men he called brothers, even though he'd gladly take a bullet for any one of them, figuring their lives were more worth saving than his own.

Maybe that was why Storm didn't like him enough to

stick around. If he didn't think he mattered, why should she or anyone else think any different?

He sat back in his seat and stared out the window, noticing how the landscape started to change. Gradually, the desert flats of Yuma gave way to hillier terrains as the train made its way toward a backdrop of mountains unlike anything Blake had ever seen.

When the train pulled into the station, Blake was glad to have Percy as a traveling companion. He made himself useful collecting up Percy's steamer trunk while Percy fetched a porter. Percy strode through the train station as if he'd been doing it every day of his life, the porter at his heels and Blake bringing up the rear, trying not to stare at the crowds of travelers.

Where was everybody going? Not only were they all dressed different, some of them spoke different as well, languages unfamiliar to Blake's ear.

"People come here from all over for the weather and the spa, for their health," Percy said, as he handed the porter some paper bills once his steamer trunk was loaded into a waiting buggy for hire. The buggy even came with its own driver.

"Good day, gents," the driver said. "Where are we off to on this fine day?"

Hearing Percy give the driver the name of a hotel, Blake bit back his impatience to find out what he came here for and head back to Bullet, where things were more familiar.

His impatience must have translated itself to Percy, who gave him an amused look. "I'll just drop my things at the hotel, and we can head to the newspaper office from there."

Blake swallowed hard and nodded, feeling like a total fish out of water. He was doing this for Storm, he reminded himself. To prove he was worthy.

Percy must have read some of what he was thinking. "It's a far cry from Bullet."

"I'll say," Blake agreed, trying not to sink into his buggy seat in an attempt to disappear. His thoughts drifted back to Storm. How had she done it?

In her short life, Storm had traveled from Ireland to New York to the town where he was now. Maybe she didn't even like Bullet. Had no urge to stay, no matter what.

"Were you surprised when Henrietta got hitched to Braydon?" he asked. Henrietta had been well-traveled also, more so even than Storm, and she had traded in her wanderlust for life in Bullet with one man. Maybe one day Storm would be willing to do the same.

"Nothing really surprises me anymore," Percy said.

"Is that because of everything you've seen?"

Percy laughed. "No, it's because of the people. No one, and I mean no one, is predictable. Just when you think you have them figured, this is how they are and how they'll always be, they turn around and surprise you. Do the exact opposite of what you expect." His gaze met Blake's with an intensity Blake found unsettling.

"Take you for example. Small town fellow. Probably never been on a train or anyplace farther than Yuma before today. Am I right?"

Blake nodded.

"All of which tells me you have some pretty powerful motivation behind your actions." Percy steepled his fingers. "Knowing what I know about human nature, usually there is a woman involved somehow, in order for a man to behave in impulsive, uncharacteristic ways."

Blake wondered if his face was giving everything away. Brody and the others had joked before about him not having what they referred to as a "poker face".

They arrived at Percy's hotel, which was grander and fancier than anything Blake had ever seen. Once he was done staring at his surroundings, he admired the smoothness with which Percy filled out the guest registry. In short order, Percy had arranged to have his bags delivered to his room and learned the location of the newspaper office.

"I can see you're champing at the bit, so we'll head there now, before we stop for a bite to eat," Percy said. "Somehow, I feel the sooner you find out what you came here for and get back on the train home, the happier you will be."

"You tell that from looking, or a lucky guess?" Blake asked.

"In order to study history, one also needs to be an observer of human nature of the time," Percy said.

Blake wondered if Percy had been making a study of him the whole time he'd been in Bullet. He figured maybe so.

The newspaper office was only a few blocks from the hotel. Percy thickened his British accent and pulled out some papers that had several people in the office running around like chickens with no heads, tripping over themselves in their eagerness to help.

In a short amount of time, Percy had learned not only the name of the rancher, but the fact that the man's wounds, while severe, had not been fatal.

Phew. So at least Storm wasn't wanted for murder.

Authorities had been unable to locate the man's wife, whom he claimed was the responsible party for his injuries. The publisher himself spoke to them, adding as an aside, that folks around here figured the bastard more than likely had it coming, citing his first wife's suicide.

Percy acted as if none of this information was a surprise,

72

nodding and interjecting comments here and there, before extending his thanks at the end of their visit.

"Nice little gal he ordered up through the mail," the newspaper fellow said. "Too nice for the likes of him," he added. "Hats off to her for up and leaving him. I'm not the only one in town who thought it was a shame he didn't bleed to death."

"Not generally very well liked, your mystery rancher," Percy said at their next stop, an elegant bar off the lobby of the hotel.

Blake looked around the room, uncomfortably aware that he was under- dressed. Shame he didn't have his marrying and burying suit on.

Percy strode forward as if he owned the place. "Come along. We'll take a seat at the bar. Bartenders tend to know everything that goes on."

Percy ordered a fancy drink, something he called a Manhattan. "It's named after the Manhattan club in New York City where it was invented," Percy told Blake. Blake stuck with a beer, all the while wondering how Percy not only knew all this stuff but remembered it.

He sipped his beer, which tasted different from the beer he was familiar with back home.

"It'll be made with different hops," Percy said when Blake mentioned the fact, trying to act like he was sophisticated and worldly-wise, at least to some degree. He tried to imagine Storm in this environment but couldn't.

She struck him as more plain folk like him, not one of these fancy city slickers. Not that Percy was one of them either. Not really. He was as down-to-earth as the next man. He was just someone who managed to fit in no matter where he wound up. Blake admired that.

Right now, Percy had engaged the bartender in a chat,

low-voiced so as not to be overheard by the other patrons. A few precise questions, an exchange of information and more paper money, and Percy finished up his drink. He glanced at Blake. "You ready?"

Blake rose from his stool. Outside, he heard the train whistle signaling an approaching train pulling into the station.

"Come on. Let's get you back onto the train and on your way before you have a heart attack from all this commotion," Percy said. He took Blake's arm and herded him through the throngs in the station, secured him a ticket, and guided him to the platform.

"Tell Storm everything is fine. That man she was unfortunately married to was recently stomped to death by a wild horse he was trying to break. A fitting end, really."

"What?" Blake's jaw dropped.

Percy clapped him on the back. "I have eyes in my head, Blake. A blind man could see the way you two have been looking at each other since she got to town. I'm just glad we didn't have to go and have a shoot-out with her nasty husband to guarantee she's a widow and able to get remarried. If she wants," Percy added. "The rest of it's up to you."

When the train started to move, he pushed Blake toward the train steps. "Away with you. You've already cut into my spa time."

Blake jumped on, hanging onto the bar alongside the steps. "I don't know how I'll ever be able to thank you," he said, as the train started to gather momentum.

"Be happy," Percy said, loudly enough to be heard over the sound of the steam engine. "That's more thanks than enough."

CHAPTER 6

Hawkes paced around Saunders's law office, agitation threatening to consume him. He picked up a stone paperweight and felt its pleasing weight in his hand. Shame he didn't have a skull to smash it against.

He whirled when the door behind him opened, then relaxed as Saunders entered.

"I've told you before, you need to make an appointment," Saunders said, as he rounded his desk and took a seat behind it. His gaze went immediately to the paperweight in Hawkes's hand.

Hawkes kept his gaze directly on his solicitor as he slowly replaced the paperweight onto the desk top. "And I told you. I don't bother with such formalities. Not with our history."

"I expect you're here about the land."

"Damn right. You find out yet who owns it?" Hawkes placed his hands palms down on the desktop and leaned in close, pleased to see a nervous tic jump near Saunders's left eye.

"It's not that easy," Saunders said.

"It oughta be, if you were any kind of lawyer."

"Whoever owns that land doesn't want it on record. Which is why it is in the name of a company."

"Find out who's behind the company."

"The sale was arranged through a firm in Tucson. I can't get any information out of them without calling unwanted attention to my interest."

Hawkes eyed the paperweight, temptingly close to his fist. It would make a satisfying crash as it flew through that fancy office window to his left. Maybe even hit somebody walking past.

Before he thought much more about it, Saunders smoothly slid the paperweight over to his side of the desk. As if that would stop him once he was of a mind.

"I smelled smoke earlier," Saunders said. "Looked like an unfortunate fire caught on those new building materials delivered to the property last week."

"Folks ought to be more careful than leave flammables lying around," Hawkes said.

"Fire like that might cause a slight delay," Saunders said. "But I doubt it will have much of a lasting impact on the project."

Hawkes shrugged. "Things keep going wrong on a building site. Might spook the builders that the place is cursed or something."

Saunders stood suddenly. "A little free advice, my friend. I suggest you focus on keeping your business partners happy. Not let yourself get sidetracked by situations like this that are unimportant in the overall scheme."

"I don't get sidetracked," Hawkes said. "And nothing I do is unimportant. You'd be smart to remember that."

~

STORM RETURNED her passengers to the Copper Moon, pulling her wagon to a stop near the ranch house that had started to feel comfortably familiar. All three women just sat there. No one moved or said a word, as if they were still in shock over what had happened.

Amanda spoke first. "Thank you for coming back for us."

"There's no need to thank me," Storm said.

"I know it delayed your plans."

Plans.

Did she even really have plans?

Earlier today it seemed of tantamount importance she leave the ranch, the town, Blake.

Given what she had just witnessed, and the way a tragedy didn't tear people apart so much as draw them tighter together, her bid to leave seemed childish and self-ish. Or was that the way she always coped? Ingrained habits of a lifetime.

After Ma died in Ireland, she and Da lit out for the new world. After Da's passing, she had followed the same pattern. Headed for the lure of greener pastures in Colorado. And when that life didn't work out the way she hoped, she had hit the road again, finding along the way, a means to ensure she never had to settle down. The book wagon gave her the excuse to be forever on the move.

"I wish I could have done more," she said. "Stopped them, somehow. Before the fire got started in the first place."

Amanda gave her hand a squeeze. "You did as much as anyone could have. More, really." Amanda watched her closely, and Storm knew her face must be a mish-mash of emotions and indecision. "Any idea where Blake went?"

"No idea," Storm said. "Has he done this before?"

"Taken off without a word? Not that I'm aware of. Laura?"

"Not as long as I've known him. It seems totally out of character."

"I hope he's all right," Storm said.

Again, that all-seeing look from Amanda. "Maybe you ought to stick around and make sure. My offer of the house in town is still good. Percy's gone. I don't like it being left empty. You'd be doing me a tremendous favor," Amanda added.

Storm felt her resistance slowly crumble. Her hands wavered on the reins she still held tight. Could she leave, without knowing for sure nothing had happened to Blake? She blew out a breath, feeling as if the decision had already been made, even if she hadn't known it at the time. "Since you put it like that."

"Good. That's settled."

As she spoke, Brody arrived and lifted his wife from the wagon seat as if she was a precious piece of glass.

"What's settled?" he asked.

Storm saw the way he rested his arm across Laura's shoulder as if reassuring himself she was all right, and that he would always be there to protect her.

She felt a tiny pang. What she wouldn't give to feel cherished like that.

She watched enviously as Laura linked her fingers through those of her husband's.

"Storm is going to stay on a while. Isn't that great news?"

"Should the boys and I start building her a cabin?" Brody joked.

Storm flushed and bit her bottom lip hard. She wasn't accustomed to the casual teasing the others took part in. "I'll be staying in town. At Amanda's house," she added.

Brody nodded. "High time someone moved here and

opened a decent hotel. If we get many more visitors, they won't all fit at Amanda's."

Storm witnessed the subtle look exchanged between Amanda and Laura. Perhaps the music hall wasn't the only new project in the works. She wondered again about the identity of the mysterious "angel investor". Sooner or later the investor was bound to lock horns with Hawkes. Brody and the others already suspected Hawkes was behind the recent fire on the site of the planned music hall.

BLAKE SPENT the return train trip to Yuma sorting things out and making himself a plan. In the past, he would have kept things to himself. But now, he didn't mind the thought of getting the others to help him. In fact, he looked forward to it. As Percy had said, that's what friends did.

He didn't know which direction Storm had headed on her way out of town, but he was confident her trail wouldn't be too hard to follow. Folks in the hick towns she visited must look forward to her arrival. Once he picked up her trail, it should be easy to figure which way she was headed next.

He claimed his horse from the livery where he'd left him, not knowing for sure how long he might be gone. He mounted up and started down the main thoroughfare with the train station, which eventually petered out at the end of town, where it became not much more than a dusty narrow road toward Bullet. Previously he'd found Yuma big and intimidating, and went out of his way to avoid the place, but compared with the hustle and bustle of Colorado Springs, he saw the town was a just another dusty train stop in

Arizona. Most folks on the train with him hadn't even gotten off here, but stayed on board for destinations farther afield.

He gave his head a rueful shake. If someone had told him, even last week, that he would have taken the train by himself all the way to Colorado Springs and back, he would have told them they were crazy. But because it concerned Storm, he suddenly felt like there was nothing he couldn't do.

He rode into Bullet, almost feeling as if the town was welcoming him home. He'd only been gone for the day, yet suddenly saw his surroundings through fresh eyes. The tidy park. The clean-swept sidewalks. Folks who lived here took pride in where they lived. Which only made Hawkes's shadowy menace all the more heinous.

He caught a whiff of smoke and burnt lumber, and wondered who'd been burning trash this late in the day.

ONCE STORM REACHED Amanda's house in town, she saw to the horses and locked the book wagon inside the barn, before dragging her few meager belongings inside.

The house was filled with items collected over a lifetime, first by Amanda's mother, then by Amanda herself. She stepped over the darker area on the carpet over near one wall where Amanda's piano used to be.

Storm knew her friend had taken her piano and her more cherished belongings out to the cabin where she lived with her new husband. She'd admired firsthand the cozy home Amanda had created with some of her favorite things, without leaving the house in town stripped bare.

She wandered from room to room, touching a lamp here, a vase there, and stroking the handmade quilt adorning the bed. The vast collection of books, Storm knew, was earmarked to be moved to help start up the new library in town.

She'd never had any possessions to get attached to. Or people, for that matter. It was hard to imagine— to look at something and know it had been handed down from your mother and her mother before her. Storm had left Ireland with little more than the clothes on her back. Her journey from New York had been the same. Fleeing Colorado had been the same again. Except for one thing. Somehow, in all her moving around, she'd clung onto the family bible. It was the one thing she had from the old country.

As she started to unpack her few possessions, the first item she pulled out was the set of scissors Blake had made her, customized for her left hand. She picked them up. As when he had first given them to her, they felt perfect, as if she had been holding them all her life.

She sighed. Twenty-two years old, and her most treasured possessions were a well-thumbed, old bible and a pair of scissors.

THE RANCH WAS a hive of activity when Blake arrived, which was unusual for this time of day. After sunset, things usually quieted right down, but everyone was still gathered in the main house when he arrived. No one even asked where he'd been, another thing that was unusual.

His first fear was that Hawkes had caused more upheaval. And that something bad had taken place. He did a quick look around and breathed a sigh of relief to see all present and accounted for. At least Hawkes hadn't grabbed up anyone, the way he'd done in the past.

"What's up?" he asked of no one in particular.

"Nothing good," Brody said. "There was a fire earlier."

"Where? Here?"

"In town. Someone tried to torch the building supplies on that vacant land."

So that's what he had smelled.

"The land where Storm's wagon was vandalized earlier?" Brody nodded.

"Seems pretty clear then," Blake said, aware all eyes were on him. For a change it didn't bother him. He had something to contribute.

"What's clear?" Brody asked, waiting.

"Someone has their eye on the land— and doesn't want anyone else near it, let alone planning to build a structure on it."

Brody gave him a slow look of approval that warmed Blake right through to his insides. "Good observation. I was too close to put it all together, but I think you might be right."

"Whoever wanted it is clearly pissed that the opportunity is gone."

"And we all know who has his mind set on buying up everything in town," Bradley said.

"Right," Brody said. "Makes it a whole lot easier to plan a defense when we know who we're up against." He leveled a look at Blake. "You take care of what you needed to take care of?"

"In a manner of speaking. But I'm going to need some help."

"Help with what?" Brody said.

"Tracking down Storm. Figuring out which way she's headed."

When the room erupted in laugher as if he'd said something ridiculously funny, Blake felt all his old insecurities resurface. He was no stranger to being laughed at. Ridiculed. Called names. Right before he was kicked and punched.

He slammed a fist onto the table. That got their attention. "It's not a laughing matter. I'm serious. I have news she needs to hear."

"You all but rode overtop of her to get here," Bradley explained. "She's holed up in town— staying at Amanda's house now that Percy's gone."

"For real?" His gaze sought Laura's. She wouldn't lie to him or laugh at him. She'd always been kind.

She reached over and patted his hand in that soft, gentle way that she had. "Looks like she might be fixing to stay a while, after all."

"But—" He'd thought it was him Storm had been desperate to get away from. "But she was fixing to leave. And never coming back. What happened?"

"Hard to say. She was right near there when the fire got started. She turned right around and came straight back here to warn us. Suddenly, she didn't seem in such an all-fangled hurry to leave after all."

Blake swallowed his impatience to head over there right now. He couldn't go banging on Storm's door this late; he'd scare the bejesus out of her. And since he'd already done that once before, sent her high-tailing from town, he needed to move more slowly this time.

"Anyone run into that reporter fellow now that Percy and Henrietta have left?" Brody asked, of no one in particular. "Is he still hanging around town?"

"I'm not sure," Blake said. "Anyone seen him around since that night he was here?" Blake saw just a few cursory head shakes. "What are you thinking?" he asked Brody.

"Just thinking out loud," Brody said. "Say that old gang of outlaws did stash the loot from their last heist somewhere nearby. Maybe you could talk to the reporter, Amanda. Tell him at least some of what your ma told you. If the reporter wrote about it, could be it would help flush out any of the old gang members that might be still alive. If we could connect them to Hawkes somehow..." He shrugged. "Like I said, just thinking out loud. Maybe it'll keep Hawkes too busy to pull any more stunts before the new music hall gets built."

"You think it was him then?" Blake said.

"Stands to reason," Bradley said. "He doesn't know we own it, yet he's still doing his level best to stop it from being built on."

Personally, Blake doubted anything would keep Hawkes too busy to spread his evil around Bullet, but he kept his doubts to himself.

HAWKES FUMED as he sat in the outer room of Fizzler's office. He was an important client. He should have been ushered right in, not kept waiting like some kind of lowlife. Finally, he heard movement on the other side of the door, seconds before the lock clicked, the knob turned, and the inner door opened. Hawkes cynically wondered if Fizzler really thought a locked door was capable of keeping him out.

"Sorry to keep you waiting, Mr. Hawkes."

"Don't make a habit of it," Hawkes snarled, as he pushed past Fizzler and plopped down into a stiff leather chair inside the inner office.

He saw a file with his name marked on it, sitting on top

of Fizzler's desk. Did the idiot really think he didn't know the amount of his loans?

"I assume you are here to make a payment?" Fizzler asked as he pulled the file toward him and flipped it open.

"Better," Hawkes said. "I'm here to grow your business for you. I need to borrow more."

Fizzler's face showed no emotion.

What was wrong with the man? He ought to be jumping up and down at the chance to soak Hawkes even more with the exorbitant interest rates he charged. When Fizzler finally spoke, it seemed he was weighing his words carefully.

"I'm afraid that's not going to be possible," the banker said. "You're at the maximum now of the amount we originally agreed upon."

"What?" Hawkes blustered. "You don't think I'm good for it?"

"It's not a matter of what I think," Fizzler said smoothly. "It's simply a matter of minimizing the risk for my investors. You've made a lot of promises, none of which has been delivered on yet. You're not showing any sort of return that would enhance investor confidence."

Enhance investor confidence.

Did Fizzler really think he could blow him off with a bunch of mumblety-peg? Who did dumb-wad think he was dealing with?

"I told you, you got nothing to worry about. I'm this close to a big wind-fall." He held up his second and third fingers entwined.

"Be that as it may," Fizzler said, "until such time as you arrive with cash in hand, there's nothing further I can do."

"Bunch a hooey," Hawkes said, leaping to his feet. "If I

had cash in hand, do you think I'd be in here asking for more?"

"Unfortunately, Mr. Hawkes, it is much easier to borrow money, when one has money. Now if you were to liquefy some of your assets, that ranch land you recently bought near yours, then perhaps our conversation would be taking a different turn."

Hawkes stormed out. Fizzler made it sound so easy. He didn't know Hawkes had already taken out several notes against the land next to his— from folks that were far less civilized in their dealings than Fizzler.

STORM WOKE UP SLOWLY, staring at unfamiliar wall paper and wondering where she was. Then it came to her. She was at Amanda's. Indefinitely it would appear. She swung her legs over the side of the bed and stood up. Had she made the right decision?

As she'd seen last night, the house was bigger and grander than anyplace she had lived before. And while Miss Millie had left Storm some bank notes along with the book wagon, Storm knew her money wouldn't last forever. She had horses to feed and care for, as well as herself. And she couldn't impose on Amanda's generosity for long. She would have to earn a living somehow if she planned to remain in Bullet.

She lit the stove and boiled some water for tea. Truth be told, the idea of staying put was a complete novelty. She shouldn't get too attached to the town or her friends here. Maybe she just wasn't the settling-down type. Maybe she was meant to be always on the move.

Funny how the idea of moving on held such scant

appeal. She wanted to be here to see Laura's and Amanda's babies after they were born. To watch the music hall get built. To help Blake with his letters.

Blake. She wondered what he would think once he found out she was still here. Surely, he wouldn't think she'd stayed on for him. He knew she was already married, and that there couldn't be anything between them other than friendship. Which did nothing to lessen the growing feelings she was coming to have for him.

Could she stay? Watch him join the trend started by Brody, with each of the Mason brothers eventually finding themselves a bride?

She sipped on her tea, figuring she ought to make a plan. Maybe she'd stop by the café. She'd never been a waitress or a cook, but perhaps Georgina would have some ideas on what she could do to support herself— as well as help fill up her days. She wasn't used to just sitting around idle.

She was just about to set out, when she heard a knock at the door. She peeked out the side window from behind the curtains. A man stood there, with his back toward her. She wondered if it was one of the men she'd seen yesterday before the fire started. What if they'd seen her in the book wagon after all, had hunted her down to ensure her silence? Maybe if she didn't answer, he'd just go away.

"Storm, it's me, Blake. The others told me you were here."

Instinctively her hands flew to her head to make sure her hair was tidy. She pinched her cheeks to add a little extra color and pasted a casual smile on her face before she opened the door.

"Blake," she said. "What a surprise."

"Not as much of a surprise as when I found out you were still here. And fixing to stay on, from the sounds of things."

"For a little while at least. After the fire last night, I don't know. It suddenly didn't seem quite so critical that I high tail it out of here after all."

"May I come in?" he asked.

"Merciful heavens. Yes, of course. I'm sorry. I must be still half asleep. Or, at least, my manners are."

Blake gave her an assessing glance as he stepped inside. "I don't seem to recall ever hearing you babble before," he said.

"You're right. I'm babbling. Please forgive me. I woke up this morning with so many questions and thoughts running through my head, it seems to have thrown me off balance."

"Maybe I can help with some of those questions," Blake said.

"Oh, dear. I don't want you to bother yourself."

Blake caught her hand, which was fluttering in the air between them, seeming to have a mind of its own. "I want to be bothered, Storm. I thought I made that clear between us before."

Reluctantly, Storm reclaimed her hand. It had felt nice clasped in his. Took away some of the lonely feeling she'd woken up with. Feeling lonely was nothing new, but it never used to bother her until recent.

She took a deep breath. There were certain things between them that needed to be said. "And I believe I made my situation clear as well," she said. "I'm either married, or I'm wanted for murder. Possibly both."

"As a matter of fact, it's neither," Blake said.

She opened her eyes their widest, and gave her head a shake in an effort to improve her hearing. "I don't believe I cotton to what you just said. I was there when it happened."

"Remember yesterday, I told you how I drove Percy to

the train station? Turned out he was on his way to Colorado Springs to, as he put it, 'take the waters'."

"At the spa?" Storm asked.

"At the last minute, I decided to go with him."

"To the spa?" Storm asked in disbelief.

Blake laughed aloud. Watching him, Storm realized she'd seldom seen him laugh. It made him look younger and more carefree, not so heavy-hearted in the way he usually did.

"Not the spa. But once we got to town, I had Percy help me do a little digging. Seems you're a widow, free and clear."

Storm's hand flew to her open mouth. "I killed him."

"Pity to tell you not. That privilege belongs to some wild horse that stomped him to death."

"Stomped him to death?" Storm echoed.

"Fitting end, if you ask me," Blake said. "Which brings me around to what I asked you earlier. Will you stay on here and marry me?"

Sadly, she shook her head. "I'm sorry, Blake but I can't."

She watched his eyes darken. Saw the shadowy return of that wounded spirit she had seen the first time she looked close— and every time since, until this morning. Now that hurting shadow was back, and she hated that she was at least partly responsible.

Her heart felt heavy and hollow and numb. She wondered if she would ever be capable again of feeling that elation she experienced whenever Blake walked into the room, even if he didn't look her way.

"You don't know me. I don't know you. We don't know each other."

"I know enough," he said stubbornly. "Enough to know I don't want you leaving. I want you here, sharing my life."

Storm noticed he didn't say he loved her. Perhaps like

her, he wasn't capable of that emotion, having grown up in a loveless void.

"I married a man I didn't know once before. I'm never doing that again."

The air between them seemed to sizzle with tension, as loud as lard over a flame. Without another word, Blake picked up his hat and left.

The door closed behind Blake with a loud finality. Once he left, she did what she always did. Hitched up the wagon and put distance between herself and her past.

She didn't really want to go to Yuma but wound up there anyway because that's where the road led. The town didn't look nearly as welcoming as Bullet. Despite it being early afternoon, she narrowly missed hitting several drunken cowpokes who stumbled off the sidewalk and lurched across the road in front of her.

The wagon sat where she'd pulled it to an abrupt halt, her hands on the reins trembling slightly. What was she doing here? She didn't have to keep running. That horrid man she'd been married to wasn't about to jump up out of his grave and assault or threaten her. She was truly free. Free to make her own life and her own way.

When she picked up the reins and started to move again, she saw she had stopped just outside a church. The front doors stood open, as if in invitation. Without conscious thought, she clambered down and hitched the horses to the post out front. It had been a long time since she'd been inside a church.

She had visited St Patrick's Cathedral in New York, where she lit candles and spent hours on her knees praying for Da to get better. Her prayers had all been in vain. And when her life in Colorado felt like hell on earth, she truly believed the Lord had turned his back on her. But perhaps those two incidents had simply been her life lessons, and she was once more in His favor.

She paused just inside the doorway as her eyes adjusted to the dim light. Out of habit, she dipped her hand into the font of holy water and made the sign of the cross before she slipped into a pew near the back. The scent from burning candle wax and the faint odor of incense were a familiar comfort.

She heard a soft step echo nearby, followed by the sound of a door as someone came out of the confessional. No one else appeared to be waiting to go next.

Slowly Storm rose and made her way into the darkened chamber. She knelt down just inside, a shadowy grate between her and the priest. Once more she made the sign of the cross. "Forgive me, Father, for I have sinned. It has been three years since my last confession."

CHAPTER 7

Leaving Storm, Blake kicked his mount into a frenzied gallop away from Bullet, away from his source of humiliation. He didn't slow until he reached the ranch, then rode aimlessly past the driveway with no destination in mind other than away. Past the ranch house. Past the spot where Percy and Henrietta had set up their camp. Past the rock cliffs and along the gorge above the river.

He stopped near the edge and stared over, down into the deep, swirling waters below. This must be close to the place where Hawkes had threatened Laura, faced off against her, rifle drawn. Laura had jumped in order to save herself from Hawkes's bullet, with Brody close behind, unaware Laura knew how to swim.

Were he to jump, the outcome would be different. He couldn't swim. The river would take him and smash him about until he drowned.

Was that what he wanted?

He turned around and headed back the way he had come. Not at all. He had a family. A responsibility to Brody and the others. A life he never even dared dream about when he was younger.

He was no quitter!

If Storm wasn't meant to share his life, he could learn to accept that. He liked doing things for her. He smiled, recalling the day he gave her the scissors he had fashioned just for her. Her boundless joy and surprise and amazement had warmed his innards, knowing that he had done something special for a special lady. Storm deserved all that. All that and a whole lot more.

Now he had an even bigger surprise he was working on for her. He'd figured on giving it to her for a wedding gift. Instead, it would be a "just because" gift.

He leaned down and patted the neck of his horse. "Good boy, Trigger. Let's go home."

He wasn't sure if Trigger understood the words or just the tone of his voice, but the horse tossed his head and whinnied as if in agreement.

Half-way back to the ranch house, Blake heard a horse and rider coming his way. Remembering what had happened to some of the others when they were riding alone, he pulled up, placed one hand on his rifle, and waited.

When he recognized John Jones, the reporter, he nudged Trigger straight into the pathway of the other party. "Hold up!"

Jones reined to a stop, just shy of running into him.

Blake eyed the other fellow. "You're trespassing, Jones. Again!"

Jones's horse seemed skittish, prancing back and forth, stirring up clouds of dust on the narrow path with its hooves, which told Blake the city fellow wasn't much of a horseman.

"Horse has a mind of its own," Jones blustered, red-faced.

"Kinda like its rider. What were you told last time we found you blundering around where you're not supposed to be?"

"I got a nose for a good story," Jones said. "I'm not resting until I find it."

Blake crossed his arms over his chest. "What story?"

"Red's Rowdies, and what happened to their last haul," Jones said.

"We told you before, you're way off base," Blake said. "There's no evidence to suggest the gang and their loot ended up anyplace near the Copper Moon."

"I disagree," Jones said defiantly.

"And you remember what Brody said. Someone might just accidentally mistake you for a wild animal going after our herd."

"I guess I've got no choice then but report my findings to the sheriff."

Blake stiffened. None of them could stomach Sheriff Yates. And Blake knew the man would jump at the chance to come sniffing around Copper Moon on any old pretext.

"Findings?" he said casually.

"I discovered what looks to be a bone. A bone that doesn't belong to any wild animal I've ever seen." Jones was boasting now— enjoying the upper hand. "I swear on my mother's grave, it's part of a human skeleton."

Blake narrowed his gaze, unsure if he should believe the fellow or not. "Tell you what," he said. "Give me a chance to talk Brody around. Stop by the ranch tomorrow morning. You can take us out and show us what you found. If your story has merit, I guarantee Brody will give you license to keep investigating. But the deal goes south if you talk to the sheriff. That sound fair?"

Jones considered only briefly. "I'll be by tomorrow at first light."

"You never know," Blake said. "Could turn out someone in the family has some information to pass on that you'll find mighty interesting. So stay away from the sheriff."

Jones smiled. "Now we're talking."

The reporter turned around and rode off whistling. Blake followed closely until he reached the driveway to the ranch house, where Jones continued on toward town.

It wasn't until after supper, when most of the others had turned in, that Blake had a chance to pull Brody aside.

"Everything okay?" Brody asked, subjecting Blake to a look he was more than familiar with. Brody's big-brother-sees-all look.

"Yes and no," Blake said vaguely, not willing to talk about Storm and her recent rejection of his overtures.

"Storm?" Brody asked.

Brody always did see through him like glass. "I guess she's the "no" part," Blake admitted.

"Remember when Laura first came back to town? What an ass I made of myself?" Brody said.

Blake smiled at the memory. "Since she agreed to marry you, it couldn't have been all bad. Besides, she still loved you from before."

"Which I was too stubborn and pig-headed to see. Let my own ego get in the way. She hurt me pretty bad when we were younger."

"But you didn't give up."

"That's right," Brody said. "I'm going to suggest you do the same. Women need to be wooed. To feel special. Don't know if they're the forever kind, but the lady has feelings for you, Blake."

Blake blew out a breath. "It's complicated."

"We all have those scars from the past. The ones that never quite go away. But they fade over time, long as you don't keep picking at the scab. Opening up old wounds."

Blake decided it was time to change the subject. "Ran into Jones, the reporter, earlier today. Trespassing again."

Brody didn't look surprised. "Somehow, I didn't figure we'd seen the last of him."

"He was threatening to go to the sheriff. Found what he thinks is part of human remains someplace out back on ranch property."

"What did you tell him?"

"I hope I did right," Blake said. "I told him not to go to the sheriff. To come out tomorrow and see you. That we might have more information for his story on Red's gang."

"That's Amanda's story," Brody said. "Don't rightly get the sense she's ready yet to share it."

"I expect she'd do anything you asked, if it was deemed good for the ranch and the family."

"What else?" Brody said.

"He agreed to show us whereabouts he found the remains, if you'll give him permission to snoop around more. You never know, Brody. He could be onto something. Gang treasure around here after all."

"There's no treasure here," Brody said. "But this ranch does seem to have its share of secrets."

"Anything to do with why Hawkes wants to get his meaty paws on the place so bad?"

As usual, Brody didn't answer whenever anyone asked him that directly. Blake studied the other man, aware Brody knew more than he was sharing. No doubt in an effort to protect the rest of them. Because protecting others was what Brody did.

JONES SHOWED up at the ranch house bright and early the next morning. "You got some stories for me?" he asked.

"Could do," Brody said. "All depends what you got to show us first."

"Oh, no," Jones said. "A good reporter never lays his cards on the table first."

Brody widened his stance, stared the reporter down. "My ranch. My rules." Blake could see Brody would be a formidable opponent at the gambling table.

Jones looked away first. "What about your word?"

"You got that as well. Now, are we going to sit here jawing all day? Or go for a ride?"

Jones plopped his hat on his head. "Saddle up, fellas."

It seemed to take hours for Jones to guide them to the cave in question. Blake had a feeling the reporter was winding them in circles and back-tracking on purpose, so they wouldn't be able to find the spot again without him. More than once, Jones pretended to take a wrong turn, which he then corrected.

Eventually, they wound up on a part of the ranch where Blake had never set foot. He doubted Brody had either.

"That's it. Just up ahead on the left," Jones said.

At his signal, the three men dismounted and continued on foot. The mouth of the cave was well camouflaged by creosote bush and mesquite. Sensing a trap, Blake was on full alert and made eye contact with Brody before the two of them followed Jones into the dark interior of what was indeed a cave. Hard to see how far back it went, but inside was too short for any of the men to stand upright.

Jones lit a lantern, and the flickering light it threw cast shadows on the rough cave walls, barely illuminating much of the area's dark recesses.

"It's back here," Jones said.

Blake unholstered his pistol, just in case. From the corner of his eye he saw Brody do the same.

"Son of a bitch!" Jones exclaimed.

Blake felt his heart kick into high gear.

"What is it?" Brody asked.

"The remains are gone," Jones said.

AFTER AN UNEVENTFUL FEW days in Bullet, Storm bolstered her courage and took herself over to the diner between breakfast and lunch. Inside was as quiet as she had hoped, and she found Georgina polishing silverware and glasses. The woman looked genuinely happy to see her.

"Is it true what I heard? You're fixing to stay in Bullet?"

"Word travels fast," Storm said.

"Amanda stopped by on her way to the building site to assess the damage from the fire. She's really pleased to have you stay at her house."

Storm glanced around, admiring the bright décor of the diner. Diffused sunlight filtered through the light, gauze-like curtains at the windows. "Those curtains are perfect."

"That was Laura's idea, on account of it'd be too hot in here otherwise," Georgina said. "Laura had a lot of good ideas when we were working on the expansion."

"You're lucky to have such nice friends."

"They're your friends too, Storm." Georgina gave her a

long look, tossed aside her polishing cloth, and gestured to the back booth. "Why don't we sit a spell? Always happy for an excuse to get off my feet."

Storm nodded, her heart pounding as she followed the other woman. Georgina stopped on her way for two cups of coffee which she set down on the table between them.

"I can usually tell when a body has a thing or two they need to get off their chest," Georgina said, without preamble. "Comes from years of working with the public."

"I sort of figured, if I decide to stay," Storm said, "that I'll need to find something to do. Keep busy and earn some money. I need to pay Amanda rent if I stay on."

"Aren't you planning to help Amanda once the hall gets built? That's what she's hoping. Laura will be too busy once the baby comes."

Obviously, Georgina didn't know Amanda was also in the family way, and Storm felt a little niggle of satisfaction that she'd been the one to earn that confidence. "I doubt a baby will slow Laura down for long," she said. "Besides I'm helping Amanda out as a favor."

Georgina looked down as she stirred her coffee thoughtfully. "I expect you're right about Laura. Never was any flies on that woman." She cocked her head. "You chat with her any, about what you might like to do?"

Storm pressed her lips together. "Not much I know how to do. Lending books and sewing is about all."

Georgina's head snapped up. "Sewing?"

"That's what I did in New York, before—" She stopped. She couldn't say before she moved away and got married. "Before my da passed and I moved out west."

"But a seamstress is just what's needed here in Bullet."

"It is?"

"I had to go clear to Yuma to find someone to make these

curtains for me. Took forever by the time they came out and measured, and then came back. Charged me extra for the travel, and even then, the woman didn't do a good job." Georgina picked one up and pointed out the uneven hand-stitching on the hem. "Hung crooked. I tried to fix them myself, but I'm no sewer."

Storm sat back, coffee forgotten, her mind whirling. Could she do it? Hang out her shingle as a seamstress and find work?

Georgina cleared her throat. "I might know someone who could help. If you need some start-up cash."

"I may have overheard something about an angel investor round these parts," Storm confessed.

Georgina nodded. "Helped me with getting things going around the cafe. Helping Amanda with her project as well. I also know when Henny gets back from her honeymoon, she's thinking on building a real honest-to-goodness hotel here in town."

"And this investor. He's willing to help women?"

Georgina laughed. "Honey, the angel investor *is* a woman."

AFTER HER TALK WITH GEORGINA, Storm stopped by the site of the recent fire. She found Amanda there, along with Bradley. Storm felt a small pang at the close way the two conferred, how Bradley deferred to his wife's observations and findings. How lucky her friend was to have found a man who supported her and helped her. Bradley had his own responsibilities on the ranch, but he still found time to assist his wife with her endeavors.

After a few brief pleasantries were exchanged, Storm

took her leave. If only she had someone with whom she could talk over Georgina's suggestion she hire herself out as a seamstress. But Amanda was totally involved in her project with the hall, and Storm didn't want to bother her.

She took her time heading home, knowing that the big, empty house would feel even lonelier than it did when she woke up each morning. Just as she reached the front steps, she spotted movement in the shadows of the porch. A man sat on one of the wicker chairs. He stood when he saw her approaching.

Blake!

She didn't know if she ought to be happy to see him or cross that he felt quite at home hanging out when she wasn't there. In the end, she decided just to be grateful for the company.

"Did you come for more letter lessons?" she asked, trying to keep her tone even and ignore the way her heart always raced around Blake.

He smiled down at her and snatched his hat off his head. "You look mighty pretty today."

"Flatterer," she said, well aware her worn, serviceable clothing was nowhere as nice as Laura's or Amanda's.

He caught her chin with his forefinger and tipped up her head. "God's truth."

She felt her lips tremble, wishing he would kiss her. He must have noticed, for he smoothed her lower lip with the pad of his thumb.

She held firm, resisting the urge to throw herself into his arms. To say she'd changed her mind. She'd love to marry him. To stay here. To belong somewhere for once in her life.

"I've been practicing with those cards you made me. I was hoping one of these days you might give me a test. See if I get a gold star." He smiled down at her as he spoke.

Her heart warmed to see the new Blake was back again. The one who looked found rather than lost. Light rather than heavy. Happy rather than wounded.

"I was thinking about what you said," he continued. "About not wanting to marry a stranger. Seems to me the best way to do something about that, is we spend more time together. Get to know each other."

She tilted her head and pulled out the door key. "You know my secrets. Are you ready to share some of yours?"

"All of them." He pulled her close. "I don't want there to be secrets between us. Ever."

She put a hand on his chest, feeling like she needed space between them. This was happening too fast. She didn't recognize this new Blake. Felt she knew him even less than she'd known the old one.

"Did something happen?" she asked.

"Lots of things," he said. "But first off, I wanted to give you this."

"Blake, you shouldn't be bringing me gifts. The scissors are wonderful but I really don't need—" She bit off her words. He'd moved to the far corner of the porch. Perched there on the side table was a sewing machine she hadn't noticed earlier because she'd been too busy looking at Blake.

She started toward it, then turned back to him. "It's too much. I can't accept it."

"You're going to have to."

"Give it to Amanda or Laura. Georgina, even."

"Won't be any good to them."

"Why not?"

"It's a special machine created for a special lady."

She looked again— sucked in her breath and blinked back the sudden rush of tears, unable to speak past the lump in her throat. Slowly she reached out and touched the gleaming black body of the machine. Trailed her fingers over the familiar housing, turned the wheel.

As the wheel turned, so did her entire life. Upside down and sideways. She threw herself at Blake, who staggered back a step as he caught her to him.

"You made it for me! You made it to work so I can sew with my wrong hand."

He caught both her hands in his between them and raised them to his lips, one at a time, while his tongue traced circles in her palms— followed up by a hot, wet kiss to each hand that set her blood singing.

"Can't see a single thing wrong with either of these beautiful hands. Hands I love as much as I love the lady they belong to. No such thing as a wrong hand."

They were so engrossed in each other, that neither of them noticed the shadowy figure, watching them from across the street.

"You did good," Hawkes told Denim, as the two rode back to his ranch. Hawkes was breathing heavy and sweating in the heat. "On all counts."

"Looking forward to that bonus you promised. Wasn't easy digging up all them bones and getting rid of them someplace they won't never be found." He shot a cunning look toward Hawkes. "How'd you know that old cave was some sort of burial ground?"

"What did I tell you about asking nosy questions?" Hawkes narrowed his gaze. "You wouldn't be going and getting greedy on me now, would you?"

"Hell, no. Done everything you tole me. Got rid of the

bones. Got rid of the reporter. Had me a little talk with the sheriff. Told him what you told me to say, just like we went over. How I seen Brody and one other idiot brother with the reporter. The really dumb one who never says much."

"Good." Hawkes pulled up short as they reached the ranch where a familiar figure waited out front. "Don Lucas. I thought you went back to Mexico."

Don Lucas gave him a look that nearabout chilled the blood in his veins. "Money and murder don't mix my friend. My investor friends are very unhappy with you."

BLAKE COULD HARDLY WAIT to get back to the ranch and report to Brody the success of his visit today with Storm. He was telling Brody and Laura all about the sewing machine, and Storm's reaction, when Bradley and Amanda burst into the ranch house.

"Sheriff's on his way," Bradley said, mouth tight, face tense. His gaze passed from Brody to Blake and back again. "Seems that reporter fellow has gone and got himself killed. And the last ones seen with him are you two."

CHAPTER 8

Brody rose and beckoned for Blake to follow him from the ranch house to his and Laura's place.

"What are you thinking?" Blake asked, once they were away from the others.

"Sheriff Yates is an idiot, as we all know. The less we say the better. We just need to come up with a plausible excuse as to why we were with Jones the other day."

"I never saw anybody else around when we were out there," Blake said. "Could be just a made-up story."

"Made up by the killer," Brody said.

"Hawkes?" Blake asked.

"Whoever was responsible, it stinks to high heavens," Brody said. "Jones tells us he unearthed some human remains. By the time we three get to where he claims he found them, they've been removed."

"I'm guessing someone didn't like Jones digging around for dirt on Red's Rowdies."

"Quite possibly so. In the meantime, we've got to come up with something to tell the sheriff when he asks."

"I just hope whoever killed Jones didn't plant something

incriminating on the body." Blake exchanged a long look with Brody as they both remembered what almost happened to Braydon.

~

"Jones came to see me a few days before he died," Sheriff Yates said. "Told me you boys had threatened him if you caught him trespassing."

"That's not quite the way it happened," Brody said. "He asked for permission to do some investigating on the ranch for a story he was working on. I told him 'no' and that was the end of it, far as I know."

The sheriff eyeballed Blake and Brody closely, as if he had some kind of truth meter hooked up to them, Blake thought cynically. Sheriff had been listening to Hawkes for so many years now, he wouldn't know the truth if it bit him in the ass.

"And there were no threats made?" Sheriff Yates said.

"No, sir," Blake said. "Heard tell he was killed in his room at the rooming house. None of us even knew where he was staying."

"But you don't deny seeing him earlier."

"Like I said before," Brody said, "Blake and I took him out to the road and showed him where the Copper Moon property extends to. Just so Jones was clear. That way he wouldn't accidentally wander onto ranch land the way he did in the past."

"Got any motive for the killing?" Blake asked. "Maybe he made some enemies back in Philly and they followed him here."

"Or maybe," the sheriff said with a dark look, "he managed to make some enemies since he's been here."

"I heard that can happen with reporting," Brody said. "Easy enough to go stirring up a hornet's nest. One other folks would rather see left alone."

"You mean like a story about the gang that used to rob the stagecoaches?" Yates said.

"Lots of unanswered questions about those old days," Blake said. "One can never really be sure just who one might be talking to, making certain folks nervous and all."

"Plenty of locals want the past left where it is, buried and forgotten," Brody said.

Sheriff gave them both the evil eye one more time before he mounted up. "You boys better not be holding anything back on me. Truth has a way of rearing its ugly head eventually."

"If we think of anything, Sheriff, we'll be sure and let you know," Brody said.

He slanted Blake another look as the sheriff rode off. "Think he bought it?"

"Dunno why he wouldn't," Blake said. "He's been buying Hawkes's bull all these years."

Brody clapped him on the back. "Never mind that. Glad to hear things went over well with Storm and the sewing machine."

Blake felt a warm flush creep up his neck. "She seemed to like it pretty fine, all right."

Brody gave a satisfied nod. "I told you a woman needs to feel special, didn't I?"

Blake blew out a breath. "I tell you. That one's going to be a tough act to follow. I'm plumb out of ideas about what I should do next."

"Maybe you ought to try just being yourself."

"What do you mean?" Blake asked.

"What I mean is, you've already fixed up her book

wagon so it's better than new. Changed up that machine so it works better for her. Pretty much the grand gestures. Maybe it's time to pull back. Spend some time with her. Listen to her. Goes a long way when a woman feels that what she has to say is important."

Blake's lips twitched. "Based on your own experience?"

"You bet," Brody said. "When Laura speaks, I listen and listen good."

Bolstered by his pep talk from Brody, Blake returned to the main ranch house where Laura and Amanda were doing something mysterious in the kitchen. He stood there, watching for a minute, before he realized they were making candles. Funny, there were always candles around, but he'd never given much thought as to where they came from.

When it appeared they were all done with the hot paraffin, he cleared his throat noisily, hoping to catch their attention without startling them.

"Blake," Laura said. "You and Brody all finished up?"

He nodded, suddenly tongue-tied. Reminded himself it was okay to ask for help. Then Brody was there with him, having his back the way he always had, since that first day they met.

"Ladies," Brody said. "I believe Blake is in need of your assistance with a certain matter of the heart."

That got their attention. They gathered around him, all excited.

"With Storm?" Amanda squealed.

"What can we do to help?" Laura said.

STORM OPENED THE DOOR, delighted to see Amanda on the other side, her arms full of clothing.

"Blake told us all about your sewing machine," Amanda said. "I'm hoping you have time to do some alterations for me."

"I have nothing but time. What do you need done?"

"I need my skirts let out," Amanda said. "Just a little for now."

"Of course." Storm relieved Amanda of her burden. "I'm happy to help." She paused, wondering how best to broach something she had been wondering about. "I noticed you haven't said anything to the others. About your condition."

"Not yet." Amanda flushed slightly. "Bradley and I thought, since I'm barely showing, and it is a little soon after the nuptials, that we'd just hold off on any announcements a while longer. Besides, with Laura carrying the first of the new line of Masons, I didn't want to take away from that by chiming in any sooner than necessary."

"That's really thoughtful," Storm said. "I can do this right now if you're of a mind to wait. Can I get you some tea?"

"I'd love a cup," Amanda said, as she pulled out a chair at the table. "I'm afraid though, that I have one more favor. This one's a lot bigger."

Storm bit back her amusement as she filled the kettle and put it over the hot spot on back of the stove. "Do tell."

"I really need someone to go into Yuma for me and—" Amanda paused. "— and kind of spy on how they do things at the dance hall there. I want to do things here even better."

"I don't know anything about spying," Storm said, hating to disappoint her friend. She picked up the first skirt and her scissors.

"Spying was the wrong word. More like go in there undercover. Pretend to be a customer."

"What kind of customer?"

"I thought maybe you wouldn't mind going there one night to take in a play. Blake said he'd go with you. He offered to go right off when Bradley and I asked him, but he's a man. He won't look at how things are done the same way as a woman would."

Storm looked up from where she wielded her new scissors, picking out the side seam of the first skirt. "Do I sense a little scheming behind my back?"

Amanda widened her eyes in mock innocence. "Heavens, no. This is just friends helping friends."

"Of course it is," Storm said. Truthfully, the idea of taking in a play with Blake was all together thrilling.

Viewing the play was only the first of the "dance hall favors" Storm found herself caught up in. Because that night at the theater, she and Blake saw a notice advertising that dance lessons were available.

"We should do that, too," Blake said. "Amanda would really appreciate knowing what that's all about and how the lessons are."

Which is how Storm found herself in Blake's arms twice a week, trying not to lead with her left foot as they circled the dance hall while the teacher barked instructions and the pianist cranked out one popular dance tune after the other.

"Is Amanda going to play the piano at her dance hall?" Storm asked breathlessly. She tried to tell herself it was because of the dance steps they were practicing, but in truth it was because this was their last lesson.

She remembered the first time she danced with Blake, at Henrietta and Braydon's wedding and how she tried not to flinch when his hand rested on her waist. Now it felt perfectly natural resting there— and like something was missing when he removed it.

"She plans to offer music lessons," Blake said. "I think

she hopes that eventually she'll have other pupils to play if there's a dance or a play."

"The hall is going up really fast," Storm said. "I can already see what it's going to look like."

Neither of them commented on the fact that Bradley had hired a part-time gun slinger he knew to patrol the property at night and make sure there were no more fires or other acts of sabotage.

"You two!" The teacher singled them out. "Quit your blathering and concentrate on where your feet are."

Blake and Storm exchanged a glance and burst into laughter. Storm put on her most serious face and forced herself to concentrate on the dance instructions, when she would far rather concentrate on Blake.

On the ride home, she slid over close to Blake on the buggy seat until her leg brushed his, and she could feel the warmth of his skin right through his britches and her skirt.

"I don't care what the teacher said. I think we looked good out there on the dance floor."

Blake nodded but didn't comment further. Storm wondered if he was relieved now that their little outings were over. The knowledge that she wouldn't be seeing him every few days sounded an empty chord inside her.

"I'm thinking about taking the book wagon out for a while," she said, finally, watching and waiting for his reaction. Wanting him to ask her not to. To say he'd miss her if she did. "Now that our lessons are all done."

"Don't you have enough sewing lined up?" Blake asked.

"I have a few projects," Storm said. "But I feel bad for my book people."

"Might have an idea about that," Blake said cryptically, but that was all he said.

"Thanks for the lift," Storm said as he reined the

carriage to a stop outside her place. She thought about asking him in, but had the sense that it would only be prolonging the inevitable.

"You're welcome," Blake said, touching his fingers to the brim of his hat. "See you around."

Storm nodded. "See you around."

LAURA SEEMED MORE than delighted to help Blake pack up a picnic. "Amanda is so busy these days I am bored clean out of my mind," Laura said, as she bustled about the kitchen, wrapping thick slices of still-warm bread in a clean kitchen towel. "You tell Storm to get herself out here and keep me company one of these days," she added. "Or better yet, send Storm here and you take Brody off someplace. Get him out from under my feet."

"I'll see what I can do," Blake promised, as he picked up the loaded basket, which felt ridiculously heavy for the two of them.

"Take her some place nice, down by the river where there's no one around," Laura said. "That's what Brody and I used to do."

Blake gave her a teasing look. "Don't tell me little Brody got his start in the world down by the river?"

Laura tossed a drying towel at him. "Blake Mason. You are incorrigible. Off with you, before Storm decides she doesn't want to see you ever again. And who could blame her?"

Storm ran a loving hand over her new sewing machine which she had set up on the dining table. After fixing Amanda's skirt seams, she yearned to do more sewing than she had orders for. To that end, she had picked up some yard goods at the general store and run up half a dozen napkins, just to see how it felt to use the machine for a larger project than just alterations. It was truly amazing!

How many years had she spent feeling different, feeling wrong, frustrated by her difficulty to master tasks that looked so easy when done by others. The napkins turned out perfect, and she was just wondering what she ought to sew next when she heard someone at the door.

Despite the destruction she had witnessed with the fire being set, she reminded herself Bullet was a nice town, generally populated by good folks. She had to stop looking over her shoulder, or jumping every time anyone knocked on the door. That horrible man she'd been married to was dead. He wasn't about to hunt her down and stick a pitchfork through her in retaliation.

She rose and headed for the door. But what about all those nice folks who relied on the book wagon for their reading materials? Was she letting them down? She honestly didn't know what to do.

Even with the new sewing machine, she wasn't sure she could pass herself off as a seamstress and find enough work here to make it worth her while. She threw the lock and swung the door open. Maybe she was better off going back to her old life.

"What if I was to tell you I don't want you to do that?" Blake spoke from where he was lounging comfortably at the front door as if he had every right to be there, one shoulder propped against the door frame, a sunny smile on his face.

Storm bit her lip. It seemed she'd been speaking aloud

again, even though she thought the words were only in her head. "Thinking out loud seems to be a bad habit one develops when one lives alone."

Blake glanced over her shoulder into the room and smiled when he saw the machine in a place of prominence. "You try it out already?'

"Works like a dream," she said. She scampered over to the table, grabbed a just-finished napkin and presented it for his perusal. "What do you think?"

"Very nice," he said. "And just what we need for our picnic today."

"Our picnic?" Storm said. "Do we have a picnic planned? Because I haven't laid in enough provisions to make us much."

"All taken care of," Blake said smugly. "Nothing you need to bring except yourself. And those new napkins you made."

She smoothed a hand down her skirt. It was plain brown and one of her oldest ones. First thing she ought to make, if she was fixing to stay, was some new articles of clothing for herself. Something feminine and pretty. She looked at Blake and realized she suddenly had a reason to want to look feminine and pretty.

Back in Colorado, she'd felt the opposite. Didn't want to wear or say anything that might call unwanted attention to her.

She stopped near the door and picked up her wide-brimmed straw hat with the saucy red ribbon. It was the only thing she could truly say made her feel pretty.

Out on the porch, she stopped short at the sight of the horse and buggy waiting for them in the street.

Blake looked exceedingly pleased with himself as he

escorted her toward it. "Laura insisted I bring the buggy. She said it was more seemly for a real date."

She searched his face, wondering if he was teasing. "Blake Mason. Are you telling me we're going on a real honest-to-goodness date?"

"Best way I know for a man and a woman to get to know each other." He helped her up into the buggy, then walked around front of it and climbed in next to her.

Storm smiled inwardly when she caught sight of the oversize picnic basket near her feet. She could truthfully say she'd never before been on a real date. She settled back into her seat. She had a feeling she was going to enjoy this one with Blake a lot.

"Where we off to?"

"Can't tell you yet. Don't want to ruin the surprise."

HAWKES BURST into the sheriff's office. "Why haven't you arrested those two yet?"

Yates pushed aside some papers on his desk. "What two you talking about?"

Hawkes stalked to the desk and leaned on it, flat-palmed, his body angled toward Yates, pleased when he saw the other man draw back slightly. "You know very well what two! Denim saw them with that reporter fellow just before he was killed."

Yates pressed his lips together. "Last time I checked the law, it requires a little more evidence than the say-so of one man against another— or, in this case, two others, before I go slapping cuffs on someone and charging them with murder."

"Since when have you ever played by the rule book?"

"Since they sent that marshal here from Tucson, snooping around. I'm doing us all a favor by making sure there's no more reason for him to come back. No one ever did solve the murder of that young girl. Yet," he added.

"You threatening me?" Hawkes said.

"Nope." Yates pulled the papers back toward him and dipped his pen in the ink well. "I'm just suggesting, pleasant-like, that you look to your own stuff and leave me to look to mine. The higher-ups don't cotton to a bunch of unsolved murders in their state. It's not like in the old days when no one noticed or cared about stepping over a dead body or two. Back then it was expected. Nowadays, we got us a bunch of do-gooders parroting on about 'polite society'. Next thing you know some coot will be giving women the vote. Can't even imagine where that might lead us to."

Hawkes left without another word. It was clear Yates had come to the end of his usefulness.

At first Storm thought Blake was heading to Yuma, and she had to swallow her disappointment. But not too far outside of Bullet, a short way past the café and the park across from it, Blake guided the horse and buggy down a nearly overgrown trail that Storm had never noticed before.

She heard the river before she saw it. Minutes later, Blake pulled the buggy to a stop near the shore. The horse turned and looked at them, as if asking, "Is this it?"

Storm looked at Blake, who suddenly appeared unaccountably nervous.

"This okay?" he asked. "Laura told me she used to come here with Brody sometimes. That no one would be around."

He cleared his throat. "But maybe you'd prefer if we went to the park. Someplace there are other folks besides us."

She placed a light, teasing hand on his arm. "It's okay, Blake. I won't try to take advantage of you. I promise."

When Blake placed both hands on her waist and swung her to the ground she felt like a real-life princess. Maybe today she could pretend to be Cinderella, dressed in something other than her normally drab clothing. Something fancy enough for a ball, that wouldn't turn back into rags at midnight.

While they ate the delicious picnic Blake had brought, Storm found herself telling Blake things she'd never shared with another living soul. He listened attentively to her story of hardship in Ireland. How her ma died birthing twins and ended up buried alongside the two baby boys who had never drawn breath.

She spoke of the nightmare sea voyage that brought her and her da to the new world. How instead of a better life in the promised land, Da just seemed to give up, to waste away right before her eyes. The later part he already knew, how she'd fled Colorado and been on the run until she met Miss Millie and learned to help the old lady with the book wagon.

"It's terrible to think that everyone I ever cared about has up and died," she said finally, once she ran out of story.

Blake laid down the chicken bone he'd been gnawing on. "Think of it like this. At least you had folks you cared about, who cared about you."

"And you never did?" she said softly. "Never once?"

"Not until I met Brody." He gave a short laugh. "At first, I didn't like it. The way he kept meeting others and bringing them back to live with us at the ranch. Like I couldn't trust any of them in case they were trying to take my place. And why'd he need those others, anyway? Him and me were enough. At least that's the way I thought."

"What changed?"

"I wasn't very nice to the others. Ignored them, hoping they'd go away. I wanted things back to the way they used to be. Then, one night, Hawkes killed the twins' older brother. We were all there. We all saw what happened, but there was nothing we could do to stop it.

"We made an oath right then and there, sealed it in blood that we would work together to bring Hawkes down. To slowly destroy the man and everything he stood for. I had to learn to trust the others, and suddenly I didn't feel so alone, knowing I was among those who believed in the same thing as me. Ever since that night, I'd take a bullet for any of them, and I know they'd do the same for me."

He shrugged. "Those other feelings started to come back when Brody met Laura for the first time. I figured things were going to change if suddenly she was in Brody's life. I was happy when things between them didn't work out— until I saw how broken up he was over it. That's when I learned it was worth making change in order to make things better."

"I didn't know Laura and Brody had met earlier."

"Years ago. She came out to the ranch once after Brody's uncle died. Kind of threw us all for a loop, but made him happy, I guess. Till it was over. Man, was he miserable! I figured if that was what falling in love did to a body, I didn't want any of it."

"And now?"

Blake lay stretched out on his side, watching her, his upper body supported on one bent elbow. "Now I see the way things are between Brody and Laura. I see Bradley helping Amanda. Even Braydon, with the way he talked

Henrietta into going back to see her family 'cause he knew something would never be quite right if she didn't. Hell, I don't want to be the bachelor uncle of the bunch. Let that be Benjamin or the twins. More good things seem to happen when you're part of a couple."

Storm let out the breath that had felt trapped in her lungs. "Is that it? You only want to be part of a couple if good things happen? Because bad things can happen as well."

"Good or bad, seems to be no matter what, it's a little better or a little less bad if two of you are going through it together."

She sat up straight and clasped her bent knees with her arms, staring out into the river. "I used to believe that too—until I married that evil man in Colorado. Getting married to him made the bad stuff that much worse. And nothing good ever happened to make things better."

She felt his hand lightly, reassuringly brush against her shoulder. How could she ever have been afraid of his touch?

"You got away. That's the good thing that happened. You made your way here. That's the second good thing I know that's happened."

Damn him! He was churning up all these feelings inside her, so many she didn't know what to do with them all. Except keep staring at the river. Maybe it could wash away some of her confusion.

"I was talking to Georgina the other day. She told me I ought to just do it. Make up a sign that says 'Seamstress', post it in the front window and see what happens."

"Why don't you?"

She angled her face toward him. "What if nothing happens? Or I don't do a good enough job and the townsfolk all get mad at me, or—"

"Ssshh." He silenced her with a finger against her lips.

"Don't be inviting those bad thoughts in, Storm. You're a good person. You've helped a lot of people, including me. I'll never be the world's best reader or anything, but thanks to you, I'll never be afraid to try."

Storm felt her heart near leap out of her chest at the look in his eyes. No one had ever looked at her that way. As if she was the most precious thing in the entire world. Suddenly the swirling feelings seemed to soften and smooth themselves out. "I guess I need you around, Blake. To remind me of all that stuff that you just said."

He drew back with a frown. "I don't want you to need me around for that. I want you to feel the same way I do. That you can't breathe without me near. That part of your soul is missing when I'm gone. That your life is all wrong without me in it."

Storm choked back a sob, but the tears fell regardless, washing away all the hurt, the pain, the loneliness, the dread. She felt as if a beautiful, unexpected sunrise warmed up her frozen insides, and made her whole.

"Please, Storm, don't cry." Blake said. "I didn't mean to make you cry."

She blinked and dashed away the tears with the back of her hand. "I'm crying because everything you said was right. I feel just the way you said. All that and more."

His smile took over his entire face. "Does that mean me and the boys should get started building another cabin for after you and me get hitched?"

"I think maybe that would be a real good idea." And she leaned toward him and sealed the promise with a kiss.

CHAPTER 9

Blake and Storm shared their news that evening at supper. Looking around the big, boisterous gathering and seeing the nods of approval and the smiles of joy coming her way, warmed Storm to the very cockles of her heart. Her happiness was further fueled by the lust-filled looks from Blake. Their kisses on the riverbank had gotten pretty steamy, and it had taken enormous self-control on both their parts to stop before things got out of hand.

Even though Storm had been married before, she wanted to do things right this time with Blake. Which meant that their wedding night would be the night they fully consummated their love for each other.

"What are you planning to do with the book wagon after you get married?" Barron asked. The twins were seated at opposite ends of the table, which made it a little bit easier to tell them apart than if they sat side by side.

"I feel a bit bad," Storm admitted. "I know there are folks out there who will miss the visits and the books I bring them. But I really want to stay on here. Georgina feels certain I can get work as a seamstress, and Blake has convinced me to give it a try. I can't do both things."

"Hey!" Bishop spoke up from the opposite end of the table. "Why don't Barron and I take the book wagon out? There's not much happening around here for a while, is there Brody?"

Brody narrowed his eyes at the twins. "Why do I feel that the two of you together, ripping around the countryside in the book wagon, is a bad idea?"

"Come on, Brody," Barron said. "You know we gave up the con game years ago. We made you a promise then, and we'll not be breaking it now. It's just our way to help out a little. Brighten up some poor folks' lives."

"Maybe even make amends," Bishop added, "for some of the fast ones we pulled on unsuspecting victims."

"The twins repentant?" Ben said. "Atoning for past misdeeds? Now I've seen everything."

Storm knew the banter between the brothers was more joking than serious. "Speaking for myself, I have no objections if you two feel like going around with the book wagon. I can map out some places to go and let you know how the lending part works. Truth be told, I'd feel a whole lot better if I knew someone was taking books around to folks who otherwise would have nothing to read."

"Great!" the twins said in unison. "Then it's settled."

Storm watched the tender way Brody reached across the table and caught Laura's hand in his own, a rueful half smile on his face as he shook his head, as if to say he couldn't quite believe this family of theirs.

Storm reached out and smoothed her hand across the back of Blake's shoulders, feeling the warmth of his skin beneath the coarse fabric. She could hardly believe this half-crazy, noisy family was soon going to be her family as well.

Overnight, Storm felt her life speed up and rush past in a blur of plans and activities. Townsfolk began dropping around with sewing requests and projects. The banns of marriage between her and Blake were read. The newly-renamed women's institute hall, formerly the music hall, was taking shape with no further incidents. There was even talk that the hall might be finished in time for her and Blake's wedding.

The twins went out overnight a few times in the book wagon, which made Storm happy, especially when they returned to Bullet with good wishes for the future from some of her old customers.

Things quieted right down when Blake joined several of the brothers on a cattle drive west. Work on their new cabin came to a grinding halt while the brothers were away. When she wasn't working on her wedding dress, Storm filled up her time at the institute hall with Amanda, sewing for clients, or visiting with Laura.

BACK AT AMANDA'S house in town, Storm carefully unfolded the delicate satin fabric she had splurged on for her wedding gown when there was a faint knock at the front door. She didn't see anyone when she looked through the window, but when the knock came a second time, she opened the door to view a slightly grubby youngster in short pants.

"Can I help you?"

"Lady at the new hall sent me to get you. Said she needs to talk to you."

"Right now?" Storm asked.

"That's what she said." The youngster avoided eye contact as he shifted his weight from one foot to the other, as if impatient to be off. "You coming?"

"I guess I'd better. Give me a second to get my hat."

The youngster raced ahead, his little feet churning up dust as he turned from time to time to make sure Storm was still behind him. When they reached the new hall, Storm thought it odd the way he darted ahead through a side doorway and disappeared.

"Amanda," she called, as she stepped into the empty building. "I got your message. Are you here?"

Her footsteps echoed on the wood floorboards as she made her way from empty room to empty room without seeing a soul. Where was everyone? No workmen. No Amanda. The building might as well have been abandoned.

Finally, after satisfying herself her friend was nowhere to be found, she returned home. Either something had come up, or Amanda changed her mind and left before she got there.

She unlocked the front door and stepped inside, then paused. The house was as still as when she had left, but something in the air felt different. Was that the odor from another human body or just the mustiness of an older house? The hair prickled on the back of her neck as she removed her hat. Slowly she moved from room to room, closely studying the contents in each, but nothing appeared to be missing or out of place. In the main room the dress fabric was draped across the table exactly where she had left it. The kitchen also appeared undisturbed, as did her bedroom.

Still, she couldn't help but remember the stories she had heard from the others. How Hawkes had broken in when

Amanda lived here and ransacked the place, looking for her secret map. Followed later by the mysterious disappearance of Henrietta's ruby earrings, one of which eventually showed up in the hand of a dead girl.

Fanciful imaginings she told herself. She was simply missing Blake. Impatient for his safe return.

~

"I WISH Brody had gone with the others," Laura confided to her over one of their many pots of tea. "He's fretful as a mother hen with no chicks to take care of."

"Well, he has you to take care of," Storm pointed out, helpfully.

"Don't remind me," Laura said. "These walls are closing in on me. Why don't we hitch up the buggy and go into town? I want to see how things are coming along at the hall. We could pop in and see Georgina at the same time. I hear she got herself one of those fancy new doughnut makers for the cafe."

"Don't you think we ought to check with Brody first?" Storm asked.

"Oh, pish-tish," Laura said. "We'll be back before he even knows I'm gone."

While Storm didn't want to get on Brody's bad side, at the same time she couldn't bear to disappoint her friend. "I'm not sure," she started to say, then immediately relented at the woebegone look on Laura's face. "Oh, all right," she said. "Who am I to deny a doughnut to a lady in the family way?"

Laura's answering smile warmed Storm clear through. What a marvelous feeling, to be the one responsible for making someone else happy.

Storm glanced skyward as she hitched up the buggy. She didn't like the look of the heavy black clouds rolling in from the west. "Maybe we ought to plan this for another day," she said. Laura ignored her and clambered into one side of the buggy, as easily as if she didn't have a now noticeable bun in the oven.

"Don't be a spoil sport, Storm. We're only going into town. It's not like we're driving all the way to Yuma, or anything."

"Thank goodness for that." Storm had heard the story about how Laura and Amanda had arrived at the bank in Yuma just as it was being robbed. How Amanda pushed Laura out of the way of a stray bullet and ended up with the bullet grazing her instead.

"Do you miss teaching?" Storm asked. Laura had been the schoolhouse's first teacher when it opened.

"Not really," Laura said. "Not with all the other projects I have in the works."

Storm slanted a sideways look at her companion. Somehow, she didn't think Laura was talking about knitting a layette for the expected arrival.

"Are you the angel investor?" she blurted out, then berated herself for having such a big mouth.

Laura just laughed, clearly unoffended by the question. "Just don't be saying that out loud around Brody."

"He doesn't know?" Laura and Brody always seemed such a close couple, she couldn't imagine Laura keeping something so big from him.

"A woman should always have a little mystery in her life," Laura said. "Brody has his secrets, and I have mine."

Which set Storm wondering what secrets Blake might be keeping from her. She'd told him everything. Hadn't she?

"Do you think Blake has any secrets I don't know about?" she asked. "I thought the reading was the big one."

"They all have secrets," Laura said. "Everyone does. Along with reasons for not sharing them."

Storm thought about the weight that had been lifted from her shoulders after telling Blake about her earlier marriage. The way he had championed her cause and set her free by what he found out in Colorado. "I don't," she said. "Not anymore."

"But you used to," Laura said, with a knowing look. "And I bet you will again at some point."

"YOU EVER WISH things could stay the way they are, instead of changing all the time?" Blake asked his three companions. They were getting set to sleep under the stars on their way back to the ranch, their money pouches full after a successful sale of this latest herd in California. "Seems they've been changing even faster lately."

"What do you mean?" asked Bishop.

"I miss this." Blake waved a hand to encompass their surroundings; the comforting flames of their slowly dying fire as it sent sparks shooting into the darkness for one final flash before they disappeared forever. Their bedrolls were laid out nearby with nothing but miles of empty countryside stretching in every direction. "I know Brody has a point about moving the cattle by rail being faster, but I miss the old times."

Benjamin lay stretched out closest to him atop his bedroll, his arms stacked beneath his head. "Things have to change. Otherwise you'd still be stuck in that orphanage getting the crap beat out of you every day."

"I guess," Blake said. "You think Brody will take to being a father?" As he spoke, he picked up his whittling, aware that in a short time he'd be married, which meant his life was about to change in ways he could only start to imagine.

"He's a natural," Benjamin said. "Look at how he's been big-brothering the lot of us all these years. Personally, I'll be glad when he has somewhere new to focus his energies."

"Amen to that," Barron said, as he rolled to his feet, and ambled off into the darkness. "Gotta take a piss," he said, over his shoulder.

"Shouldn't have had that last beer," Bishop called after his twin.

"You two miss your old life?" Blake asked.

"Some," Bishop said. "Wouldn't go back to those old ways, but it's been nice to get out with Storm's book wagon, meet some new folk."

"Without fleecing them out of their life savings, you mean?" Ben asked.

Bishop threw an empty bean can Ben's way. "Pretty sure, your own past isn't exactly without a few misdeeds you might rather forget about."

Benjamin merely grunted.

"Yeah," Blake said. "What was it you did before you hooked up with Brody?"

"None of your business," Benjamin said.

Just then Bishop jumped to his feet. "You hear that?"

"Hear what?" Blake asked.

"Barron. He's been gone too long."

They all paused to listen and heard a faint scuffle in the darkness.

"Must be him now," Blake said.

Bishop squatted back down slowly, his eyes staring into the inky blackness. "Barron. That you?"

"Not exactly."

They all turned to see a stranger approach from behind, Barron locked against him with one arm, while his other hand held a pistol against Barron's temple.

"Let's everyone be all calm and friendly," the stranger said. "And nothing happens to your friend here. Do anything stupid, and he dies."

Blake froze. His heart beat double time in his chest.

"You there." The stranger indicated him. "Put down that knife you're holding nice and slow. Toss it over by the fire."

Blake did as he was told.

"That's the way. Been following you boys ever since you got off the train. Appears all that cash you're carrying is weighing you down. Happy to help out with that. Relieve you of your burden, so to speak."

Before Blake even knew what happened, a shot rang out and the stranger fell to the ground, his open eyes staring blankly upward.

Barron turned to Ben. "You cut that one a little close to me, brother."

Benjamin shrugged and put down his gun. "Got the job done. Next time be more careful where you go piss."

AMANDA WAS DELIGHTED with Storm and Laura's visit to the hall, and happily showed off the way the work crew was putting the finishing touches to the inside rooms.

"It's beautiful," Storm said, admiring the richly-polished floor boards of the main room, earmarked to be a dance hall and performance theater. The walls stretched up two floors high, making the room appear much larger than it really was.

"We brought the books from the house over to the library side," Amanda said. "But I'm not setting anything up until you're here to help me."

"Just let me know when you're ready." As they moved about the newly-constructed building, Storm noticed Laura was beginning to look tired. "We should head back," she said abruptly.

"Not until I get a doughnut," Laura said.

Storm made eye contact with Amanda, who gave an imperceptible nod before she spoke. "I'll run over to the café and pick up a few for you to take back with you."

It took longer than Storm anticipated to see Laura to the privy and back into the buggy. Luckily Amanda came rushing up at that same moment with a parcel wrapped in brown paper and tied with string. "Georgina insisted on cooking them up fresh, so they're still warm," Amanda said, as she handed the packet to Laura. "Drive safe," she told Storm. "I smell rain."

Storm did, as well. Years of driving around the state in the book wagon had taught her to stay off the roads at the first hint of heavy rain. Monsoon season in Arizona was not something to mess with.

As they started off, fat raindrops began to fall, gathering force until the rain looked like one solid sheet of water. The Copper Moon ranch had never seemed so far away as it did now. Rain lashed at them from every side. The flimsy canvas roof did little to help keep them dry, and in minutes she and Laura were both soaked to the skin.

As the rain intensified its assault, the roadway beneath the buggy's wheels turned into a mud bath. Rivulets of rain water that the dry ground couldn't absorb ran down deep gullies on either side of the road. They were near Hawkes's spread when Storm reined the buggy to an abrupt halt.

"What's wrong?" Laura asked.

"Wait here." Storm climbed down. Her heavy, wet skirt clung to her legs with every step as she inspected the roadway ahead. As she suspected, it was washed right out. From her vantage point it was impossible to tell if she was staring at a large, shallow puddle, or a deeper hole they could easily get stuck in.

She turned to where Laura sat. Her friend resembled a drowned rat. If it was just her, she might attempt it and pick her way through slowly, leading the horse and buggy. But Laura was precious cargo and her responsibility.

She sloshed her way back to the buggy and climbed into the driver's seat. Without a word, she started to carefully guide the horse and buggy in a half circle back toward town.

"Where are we going?" Laura had to yell to be heard over the loud pounding of the rain hitting the buggy's roof. The wind whipped around them in a frenzy, lashing them with sheets of rain.

"Road's washed out," Storm said. "We have to go back to town."

Laura grabbed her arm. "I need to get to the ranch," she said. "Brody will be worried."

"Sorry," Storm said, biting her lip in concentration. "We can't risk it."

"But we're almost there. That was Hawkes's place back there."

The black storm clouds that had filled the sky earlier blocked out all hint of daylight. Storm just hoped she could get them back safely to town.

~

"You're getting water all over the floor," Hawkes growled at his rain-soaked visitor.

"Worst storm I've seen in these parts," Denim, Hawkes' foreman, replied unapologetically. "Get the greasers to clean it up after I'm gone."

"What's so all-fired important, anyway? Now that that nosy reporter has filed his last story."

"Just saw Brody Mason's brood mare."

"Another Mason on the way for us to take care of," Hawkes spat out.

"Yeah, well, appeared as her and another one of them nosy gals, the one with the book wagon, were headed toward the ranch. Me and the boys dug up that chunk of road like you told us to. Sorry to tell you, the gals didn't try and drive through the washout, but turned around and headed back to town."

"Damn!" Hawkes said. He'd been hoping for a nice, tidy accident to take care of Mason's woman. The approaching storm had looked like the perfect opportunity. "Who's watching them?"

"Haywire," Denim said, referring to his somewhat-crazed, hired muscle. Hawkes was hard-pressed to tell which of the two was more loco in the head.

"You got that dynamite ready to go like I told you?"

"Sure do."

"Good." Hawkes nodded. "Then you know what to do next."

Battered by the monsoon, Blake and his brothers pressed on, glad they weren't driving a herd back in this weather. The expansion of the rail line made it much easier to transport a herd west, but coming back, it was faster to get off the train at the border and travel the rest of the way on horseback.

Home had never looked so good. Blake angled a quick, admiring look toward the almost-finished cabin where he would soon be living with his bride. Life had never felt so good. And even though he was cold and wet and the roads were bound to be a mess, he couldn't wait to reach Bullet and see Storm. He had missed her more than he would have thought possible.

He followed Benjamin and the others into the ranch house where they found Brody pacing in circles, fit to be tied.

"What's up?" he asked, finally. Brody hadn't said a word when they arrived, not even when Benjamin had revealed the size of their haul for the sale of the cattle.

"Damn woman of yours," Brody said, darkly.

Blake stiffened. His gut clenched. "What about Storm?"

"She took Laura into town is what she did."

"Is that all?" Blake willed his racing heart to slow back down to normal. "I hardly think she forced Laura against her will."

"Laura shouldn't be jostled about in a buggy on these roads. And she sure as heck shouldn't be out when there's a monsoon happening."

"Storm's smart. They'll be holed up someplace snug. She knows better than try to travel in this."

Brody shook his head. "Not so sure about that. Laura knows I'll be worried. She'll move heaven and earth to get back here."

"If Storm didn't think it was safe, there's nothing Laura could say to change her mind. I'm sure they're fine." He looked out the window. "Rain's letting up, for now. Want you and I to head into town? Make sure they're all right?"

Brody rose. "Damn straight. Was heading that way when you all arrived."

"I'll get a fresh mount."

Some miles down the road, they reached the washout. The water was moving fast, heading toward the river.

"How deep you think that is?" Blake asked.

"Too deep for a buggy to make it through safe," Brody said.

With quick, economical movements, the two men lashed their horses together in preparation for crossing. Brody went first, because that's just what Brody did. Always looking out for the rest of them.

Blake took a deep breath, said a short prayer, and tightened his grip on the reins as he followed the lead horse. He felt his horse hesitate as the water grew deeper and rushed up around his belly. He could feel the horse's hooves slide several times trying to find solid ground on the slippery bottom.

The thought of seeing Storm kept his mind clear of others things, and at long last he joined Brody on the other side.

"Look here," Brody said.

Blake squinted down at the muddy roadway. The rain had washed away most of the wheel marks, but in the deep, water-filled ruts he could make out barely discernible signs that a buggy had been there earlier and turned back around. "Looks like you're right," he said. "They did try to make it to the ranch."

He followed Brody's gaze to Hawkes's driveway. "They wouldn't go near there," he said. "They would have gone back to town."

"I just pray as they made it safe," Brody said grimly, tugging on the reins and giving his horse his heels.

Blake didn't say anything, but he knew what Brody was thinking. Seemed a pretty big coincidence to have the washout happen so close to Hawkes's place. Could have been a trap. Which didn't make a whole lot of sense. If Hawkes was after an altercation with the Masons, there were easier ways to make that happen.

He urged his horse faster.

THE RAIN HAD EASED up some by the time Storm and Laura reached Bullet. The black clouds continued to move east, allowing the sky above them to lighten. "We should have kept going," Laura said fretfully. "We'd be back at the ranch by now and Brody would know we're all right."

"Continuing on was too unpredictable," Storm said. "This way we're safe. Once we've got you fed and into some dry clothes, we'll take another run at reaching the ranch. I'm worried about that washout though. It looked deep."

"Suspiciously deep," Laura agreed. "Considering where it was on the road."

"You mean by Hawkes's," Storm said. "Blake told me the men have a long-term plan to ruin him."

"It all started before I knew Brody," Laura said. "I just wish it was over. Hawkes has got away with murder more than once. He thinks he's above the law."

"Do you think he killed that reporter?" Storm asked.

"Blake told you about that, did he?" Laura said. "All I know for sure is anytime anything bad happens in these parts, it usually has Hawkes's hand in it one way or another. I just don't understand why Hawkes would care about a decades-old story about some stagecoach robbers."

"You said it yourself," Storm replied, as the house where she was living came into view. "Everyone has their secrets."

BLAKE AND BRODY reached Bullet in record time without further incidents. Down off the end of Main Street, the new hall towered over the other establishments, two stories high, newly milled wood siding all damp and shiny in the aftermath of the storm.

Blake slowed long enough to give the building an admiring look, wondering if he was gazing at the site of his upcoming wedding. "Looks good."

"Did you hear what Amanda's planning on naming it?" Brody asked.

"I thought it was some sort of music hall, with plans to also hold community events. That's what I heard."

"That was the original idea. It's kind of changed over time. Amanda decided to call it the Bullet Women's Institute."

Blake frowned. "What's that supposed to mean?"

"Gets me," Brody said. "But if it makes the ladies happy, I'm all for it.

"Café looks like it's doing a good business," Blake said as they rode past. "Even with the storm."

"Expanding was the smart thing for Georgina to do," Brody said. "Place is far busier than in her parents' day."

"Times change," Blake said. "Georgina figured out to change with them." Which didn't mean he couldn't still feel a nostalgic twinge for the old days. Although in times past, you'd never see a woman traveling around in a book wagon.

Which meant he and Storm never would have met. So there was something to be said for progress.

Along with leaving the past buried. "Think we might try to find out what happened to the human remains that reporter fellow claimed he found?" he asked.

"Maybe after we deal with Hawkes once and for all," Brody said.

"I know you have a plan, Brody. When are you going to let the rest of us in on it?"

Brody smiled, as if to admit he'd been caught out. "When the time is right." Blake didn't miss the deft way Brody changed the subject. "Guess your wedding is coming up pretty soon. Got any pre-wedding jitters?"

"Heck, no," Blake said. "When something's right— it's right. Wasn't it that way for you and Laura?"

"A little rockier for us," Brody said. "Given that things didn't get off to a very good start."

"She wouldn't have come back if she didn't still love you."

"Took me a while to wrap my head around that. My ego was pretty bruised."

"Good thing then, that I don't have an ego," Blake said, half-joking, half-serious.

Brody let out a frustrated sigh. "I just wish Laura would listen to me, more. If she had, we'd all be safe at the ranch right now." He turned to Blake. "What do you think about the twins taking the book wagon out from time to time? What'll happen if Storm decides she wants to do that again?"

"Guess I'll be going with her," Blake said. "I sure as hell won't be letting her drive around heaven-knows-where by herself."

Brody gave him an admiring glance. "It's good to hear

you say that. Means you love her enough to put her wishes first."

"Heck," Blake said. "Never had a woman's wishes to consider before this. Feels kinda nice. Feels right somehow." He warmed at Brody's approving nod.

Minutes later, they reached the road where Amanda's old house stood, second one down the block. Suddenly Blake couldn't wait to see Storm. It felt like he'd been away for months instead of weeks. Alongside him, he felt Brody also pick up the pace, as if he felt the exact same way. He bet the two of them were grinning like fools at the thought of seeing their women.

Abruptly, an earth-shattering explosion ripped through the air. Blake stared in disbelief at the crater in the ground, littered with debris that seconds earlier had been Amanda's house. His horse spooked as the air around them grew thick with black smoke.

Blake leapt off his horse and ran to where flames greedily consumed the few walls left standing.

CHAPTER 10

Blake moved toward the devastation in a daze, barely aware of the chaos around him as neighbors rushed toward the burning building carrying buckets of water. He was jostled from all sides, but kept moving with grim determination past the brigade of men, women, and even children as they began passing buckets of water to help douse the flames.

Blake's ears still rang from the blast of the explosion as he made his way like a sleepwalker through the crowd, his disbelieving gaze fixed on the smoldering remnants. His eyes and throat stung from the smell of ruin. He felt his arm grabbed from behind and turned to face Brody, who looked every bit as shattered as he felt.

"They weren't in there." Brody's voice sounded like it came from inside a cave.

"How do you know?" Blake had no idea how his tongue formed the words. Or if they were whispered or shouted. He felt as if parts of his body had shut down. He was aware of the heat from the flames but didn't connect it with anything to do with Storm.

"I just know," Brody said.

Brody yanked Blake back, just as a piece of burning wood fell to the ground, right where he'd been standing a second earlier. A nearby man tossed a bucket of water onto it. Blake heard the wood sizzle as the water doused the flames and steam rose from the charred lumber. He continued to stare at the carnage, his insides as raw and charred as what was left of the building.

Despite the efforts of the brigade, the hungry flames jumped to the house next door, where they continued their wanton destruction.

The volunteers shifted their energies to the new fire, leaving Blake and Brody alone to stare blankly at the still smoldering pile of rubble— all that remained of Amanda's family home.

When Brody tried to grab his arm a second time, Blake shook it off. Brody took hold of him, fingers biting into his shoulders, his face inches away from Blake's.

"Snap out of it, Blake. You're no good to Storm like this."

"She's gone," he said dully. "The one person who knew me and loved me, in spite of everything."

Brody's voice rang with disgust. "You don't deserve her."

The words got through to Blake. His head snapped around. Anger, clean, healing anger, burned through him as sure as those flames had burned through the mess left behind from the explosion.

"Maybe I didn't deserve her. But she didn't deserve this. To die like this."

Brody shook him so hard his teeth rattled in his jaw. "Look around. Do you see the buggy the girls were driving? No! I tell you, by the grace of God, they weren't here when it happened. They're someplace safe, and I aim to find them. With or without you."

Blake felt the dark shroud lift from his soul. He straightened. Eyed Brody straight on. "Maybe I didn't deserve Storm, but I'm going to take care of Hawkes so no one else has to go through this kind of hell."

"We're doing that together, Blake. We swore an oath. There's power in numbers."

"Number seven," Blake said.

No sooner did the words leave his mouth, than he heard a familiar cry. He turned to see Storm jump down from the buggy and race toward them. His entire world grew bright. Except Storm rushed past him as if he wasn't there, straight to Brody. Blake froze. Did she not see him?

As if from a great distance, he heard her speak. "Laura's at the café. I'm not sure, but she might be in labor."

"Who's with her?" Brody asked.

"Georgina. She sent someone from the café to fetch Doc Parsons."

"I need to be with her. I'll meet you and Blake at the café."

Message delivered, Storm turned to Blake and moved into his arms. She ran her hands over his face in that way she had, as if she was memorizing his features by touch. "I was worried about you," she said, her words as soft as her touch.

Blake swallowed thickly and pressed his face against the top of her bare head. Her hair was damp and smelled like flowers, a whiff of sweetness amid the smoke and the ruins. "You were worried about me?" He gestured toward the ruined building with one hand, his free arm holding Storm close. "When I heard the explosion and saw the flames, I thought you were inside." He rested his cheek against the comforting softness of her hair. "I felt as if I died at that exact same moment."

"We stopped at the café to get something for Laura to eat and borrow some dry clothes from Georgina."

Blake shuddered, smoothed his hands across her shoulders to make sure she was really there. He had come so close to losing his love. "That's good," he said. "That's really good."

"Laura said she was hungry, but when she started to eat, that's when the pains started. Georgina and I were trying to make her comfortable when we heard the explosion."

"I'm sorry you lost everything," Blake said. "I'll make you another sewing machine."

"There's no need," Storm said. "It's at the café, where I was working on fixing the curtains." She gazed sadly at the destruction. "It's Amanda who lost everything. All her mother's things. So much sentimental value." She sighed. "All I lost was a few dreary pieces of clothing that I was planning to replace."

"I'll buy you all the new clothing you want," Blake said. "Anything you want."

"Why, Blake Mason. Am I marrying a rich man? I had no idea."

"I do okay with my share from the sale of the herd. But as long as I have you, I truly am the richest man in the world."

She stood on tiptoe and linked her arms behind his head. "You'll always have me."

He leaned in for a kiss. Her lips were warm, welcoming him back after what felt like a long absence.

"Luckily the book wagon is out at the ranch where the twins left it," Storm said. "And Bradley had already moved Amanda's books from the house to the hall."

"I guess Amanda can always rebuild if she wants to."

Without moving from his embrace Storm spun to face

the neighboring house, where flames had completely eaten through the roof and the trusses. "Amanda said that the house next door had been unoccupied for a while now. That's why she didn't like leaving hers empty as well."

"I'll go see if I can help put out the flames," he said. "Promise me you won't disappear on me."

"Never, my love." Once more, she touched his face. He felt the warmth of her love spread all the way through to his heart and his soul.

THINGS at the café had calmed down by the time they reached its doors. Storm was relieved to hear the doctor had declared Laura's pains to be Braxton Hicks, a false alarm, and returned to his office. Laura was sitting cozied up next to Brody, who held her as if he would never let her out of his sight again.

Laura gave Storm a look of chagrin. "I've been officially grounded. No more tearing about. Bed rest only, until this little one decides it's time."

Georgina fetched Storm and Blake some sweet tea. "You both look like you could use this."

Storm took hers gratefully. "Poor Amanda," she said sadly. "Her family home and everything in it destroyed." She hoped the shock of the news wouldn't have an adverse effect on the baby Amanda carried. She wondered if the others knew yet.

She looked up in time to catch the dark look that passed between Brody and Blake. "What?"

Brody took his time answering. "This has to be Hawkes's handiwork."

"I don't understand. What was in the house that he wanted to see destroyed?"

Blake and Brody both answered at the same time. "Our women!"

Storm blanched. "Us? We're no threat to him."

"But *we* are," Brody said. "Which means everyone we care about is in danger from that man."

"He's an evil one," Georgina said, as she fetched more tea. "Saw that the first time I laid eyes on him. And I wasn't much more than knee-high to a grasshopper at the time."

Blake pulled Storm close. "I'll never let anything happen to you, Storm. Not as long as there's breath in my body."

"I take it everybody else is safe at the ranch?" Georgina said, a wistful tone in her voice.

Georgina must be lonely, Storm thought. "Why don't you close up and come back with us?" she said, impulsively. "I'm sure the boys will have lots of stories about their trip."

"Maybe another time," Georgina said. "I need to be here in case any of those still fighting the fire stop by later."

Brody rose. "I need to get my wife back, make sure she obeys doctor's orders. Okay if I take the buggy, Storm? Think you can handle Phoenix?"

Storm tapped Blake on the arm. "I am pretty sure if I can handle this fellow here, one well-behaved stallion should be easy-peasy."

AMANDA WAS FAR LESS BROKEN up by the loss of her family home than Storm would have expected.

"I took everything I cared about with me when Bradley and I were married," she said. "I actually wondered what I was going to do with the place once you and Blake were married and you were no longer staying there."

As she spoke, she smoothed a hand over the slightly rounded bump near her waist.

Shortly after the fire, Amanda and Bradley had announced their good news to everyone, following the family supper. At which time Storm insisted both women be her bridesmaids, family way or not. *After all*, she had said, *weddings are all about families.*

"But there was some lovely furniture and things."

Amanda shrugged. "Things can always be replaced. Now let's talk about something more important, like your wedding."

Storm was working on her wedding gown, which she took out during the day when Blake was at work on the ranch, and tucked out of sight before he got back. It felt a little funny staying in Brody's old room in the ranch house, but their cabin was close enough to being finished that Blake was staying there before the wedding.

Amanda fondled the fabric. "This is going to be beautiful, you know. You are an amazing seamstress."

Storm smiled. "So much easier when one has the right tools." She picked up the scissors Blake had made for her and snipped a few loose threads.

"I'm so happy you're going to be married in the institute hall after all," Amanda said. "It's the perfect way to introduce the facility to the townsfolk."

"Well, it makes good sense," Storm said. "After all, it's still monsoon season. And as we know, anything can happen in a monsoon."

She poked her thread through the eye of the needle. "Are we sure Henrietta and Braydon will be back in time?"

She'd optimistically started to sew an attendant gown for Henrietta, as well as the other two.

"They'd better be," Amanda said. "Didn't Blake choose Braydon as best man?"

"That's the plan."

"He's starting to sound like Brody," Amanda said. "The man with a plan."

Laura arrived, carrying her new bundle. "Is this a hen party? Can anyone join in?"

"Should you even be out of bed yet?" Amanda fussed around, fetching a comfortable chair for Laura and baby Charlotte.

"I can only rest so much," Laura said, smoothing the golden fuzz on the top of her baby daughter's head.

"It was nice of her to make an appearance before the wedding," Storm said. "I only wish she was old enough to be a flower girl."

"Poor Brody." Laura chuckled. "He almost fell over when the midwife told him it was a girl."

"Surely he knew there was a fifty-fifty chance. Not very good betting odds for a man who's so skilled at the card tables," Storm said.

"Those days are in his past," Laura said.

"Did he say that for sure?" Amanda asked.

"Not exactly," Laura said. "He agreed to only hit the card tables in times of dire emergency."

Amanda nodded. "Knowing those boys, nearly anything could be considered a 'dire emergency'."

"You look tired, Brody," Blake commented as they worked side-by-side, digging the potatoes.

"You just wait until you're a new father. Every time you close your eyes the baby opens its mouth and wails." But he grinned as he said it, and Blake knew fatherhood was sitting very well indeed with his friend.

Once the crop was safely stored in the root cellar and they were washed up, Blake and Brody headed toward the ranch house. They were almost there when they were nearly mowed over by the book wagon as it came hurtling down the driveway toward the house, where it came to a stop a few feet away.

"What the—?" Brody said.

Bishop leapt from the driver's seat. Blake and Brody exchanged glances. "Where's Barron?" Brody asked.

"He's in the back," Bishop said. "With our stowaway."

Just then they heard a loud kicking and caterwauling from the back of the wagon, followed by a few succinct curse words.

Blake bit back a smile. "Someone stowed away on you?"

Bishop took off his hat and ran a hand through his hair. "That's not even the half of it. First, she tried to steal the wagon right out from under our noses."

Blake joined Brody in a huge guffaw of laughter. "Someone tried to grift the grifters? What was it? Payback time?"

"It's not funny," Bishop said. "We didn't know what to do with her. Didn't dare turn our backs on her. Couldn't just leave her on the side of the road." As he spoke, he rounded the wagon and removed a bar holding the back door closed.

"You locked Barron in there with her?"

"Had to," Bishop said. "I only hope she didn't hurt him too bad."

Brody and Blake exchanged another look, well aware

that Barron had been a champion boxer in the days before the twins joined the family.

The second Bishop removed the bar, the wagon's rear door burst open. Barron tumbled out, closely followed by a scruffy individual in tattered, oversize men's clothing. Barron threw himself atop the newcomer, flipped her onto her stomach and straddled her middle to hold her in place. The woman beneath him flailed and kicked like a lioness, as Barron raised a hand to where fresh scratches cut across one cheek.

"Merciful heavens!" came Storm's voice.

Blake figured the ladies must have heard the ruckus, for Storm burst from the ranch house with Amanda on her heels and Laura close behind. Hearing a female voice, the woman beneath Barron stopped fighting. She pushed herself onto her elbows and faced them, her big blue eyes filled with tears. "Please help me. I need to find my sister."

Laura took charge of the situation. "Barron, you get up off that poor wee thing this minute. Help her up."

With a slight glower, Barron did as he was told, then stepped back out of range.

Laura approached her and took the girl's arm. "What's your name, sweetheart?"

"Rose," she said. "And my sister's name is Lily."

"Well, you're safe here. You're among friends."

"Did you catch sight of that gal who showed up with the twins?" Blake asked Benjamin a scant week before the wedding. Seemed to him as if time sped right up as the big day approached.

"She's a looker," Ben said. "No wonder the twins didn't fall for her disguise, pretending she was a boy."

"And trying to rob them in the bargain." Blake still grinned at the thought of it.

"Hear tell she stowed away in the back of the book wagon. And that they didn't find her till they reached Bullet," Ben said.

"That was *after* they caught her trying to steal the wagon." Blake and Ben exchanged a grin at the thought of a slip of a gal putting one over on the twins. Served them right, given all the cons those two had pulled on unsuspecting victims in the past.

"I heard Georgina gave her a job at the café," Blake said. "Guess she bought the gal's sob story about looking for her missing sister."

"Georgina's got a big heart that way," Ben said.

"I sure hope Braydon and Henrietta make it back for the wedding," Blake said. "Otherwise you'll be stepping up as best man."

"Second choice, am I?" Ben grinned to show there were no hard feelings. "I'm not worried. I doubt anything could keep Braydon away from seeing you get hitched. Besides, isn't Henrietta supposed to be a bridesmaid? She'll make sure Braydon gets here in time."

BULLET'S newly opened Women's Institute was decorated with masses of fall flowers that Blake had ordered in from California. The new-building smell of fresh-cut lumber was overlaid with the heady fragrance of dahlias and chrysanthemums in every color of the rainbow.

Blake stood at the front of the hall's main room, lined up

next to his brothers, watching as the guests wandered in, exclaiming over the building before finding seats on the hastily constructed benches.

Directly across from where he and the brothers waited, Amanda's piano, moved from the ranch, held a place of prominence at the front of the large room. Amanda sat behind the instrument, her fingers coaxing a soft, lilting melody from the keys. Once the bride made her appearance, Amanda would trade her piano bench for her bridesmaid bouquet and take her place alongside Henrietta and Laura. Georgina sat in the front row with little Charlotte tucked safe against her bosom.

Next to Georgina sat her new protegee, the girl with the flower name. Rose, Blake thought it was. Tall but slim, with blond hair, the gal cooed over baby Charlotte in Georgina's arms.

Abruptly the music changed to the bridal tune that was now familiar to Blake's ears. Henrietta and Laura came first, followed by Storm.

Blake felt his heart stop, then start up again double-time. His bride was a vision in a shimmery gown of white satin that looked alive, as the light reflected on the hundreds and hundreds of sequins. He hadn't known till now what a sequin was, but he'd kissed every one of the pin pricks Storm had suffered while she sewed them on.

Storm walked toward him, alone, the way Blake knew she had walked for most of her life. But not any longer. As long as there was breath in his body, Storm never, ever would find herself alone.

Rose sat, entranced by the sight before her as the wedding got underway. The shiny new hall was decked in flowers, the likes and colors of which she had never seen before. The scene was vastly different from her old life. She glanced around, still getting used to the unfamiliar feelings she had experienced since arriving in Bullet. Feelings that came from finding herself surrounded by folks like Georgina. Folks who genuinely cared for each other.

The twins had fooled her at first, but not for long. She knew Barron to be the bolder of the two. Bishop was more of the thinker. Barron chirped up impulsively, while Bishop thought things through and spoke more slowly. Already, Bishop had claimed a special place in Rose's heart. If anyone could help her track down her sister Lily, it was Bishop.

Thanks for reading *Blake's Bride*. You might not know how important reader reviews are, but they mean a lot. Just a short sentence saying you enjoyed the book goes a long way with new readers and puts a smile on this author's face.

Review wherever your purchased *Blake's Bride* or on Goodreads or BookBub.

And please keep in touch

Website: KathleenLawless.com
Facebook: facebook.com/kathleenlawlessnovels
Instagram: instagram.com/kathleenflawless
TikTok: tiktok.com/@kathleenflawless

If you haven't already done so, sign up for my VIP Reader's Newsletter and be the first to hear about free books, fan-priced sales, and my new series. http://eepurl.com/bVosb1

Keep reading for a preview of Seven Brides for Seven Brothers, book 5, *Bishop's Bride*.

Dear Reader

The American West in the last half of the nineteenth century offers my heroines a chance to assert their independence and also introduce them to a hero who is their match in every way. My characters have their own ideas of right and wrong, good versus evil, and deal with it on their terms. It wasn't called the Wild West for nothing. Life was about conquest, survival and persistence,

I love writing a historical genre where the reader, by the simple act of picking up the book, instantly suspends disbelief. She easily forgets about her world and her woes in a tale where no one needs to empty the dishwasher or take out the trash, and adventure lies around every corner.

As an author, it's fun to carry her away to a time and place where anything could, and often did, happen. The customs of the day and the manner of dress might be different from today's world, but people are still people. They laugh, love, hurt and heal. Celebrate and mourn. They live life large. And in the untamed wildness of the settling of the west anything can happen.

Read on for an excerpt from Book 5, *Bishop's Bride*.

After the ceremony, Bishop sipped on his beer and watched the crowd, ever vigilant, as he knew the others would be as well. Which was the only way to be as long as Hawkes walked free.

He whirled when he felt someone tap him on the shoulder. How had Rose snuck up on him like that? And how had she ever fooled him, even for a second, with that boy garb she had been wearing when they first crossed paths? She stood taller than most women, willowy rather than curvy, but still unmistakably female with a trim waist flaring to slightly rounded hips beneath her simple blue gown. Her pale blond hair was pulled back from her smooth, high forehead and fell halfway down her back in soft waves. "Can I talk to you, Bishop?"

"I'm Barron," he drawled, in a deliberate attempt to discomfit her.

Her gaze on his never wavered. "No, you're not."

He blew out a breath. How was it she was the only one he could never put one over on? Him and Barron had been confusing folks since the day they were born. The only other person who could always tell them apart was their brother Joe. Right up till the day Hawkes killed him.

Her gaze moved over his face with a scrutiny that unnerved him, almost as if she was peeling back the skin and having a look inside at the inner workings of his brain. It was spooky. He crossed his arms over his chest. "So talk."

To his surprise, she tucked her hand through his crooked elbow, forcing him to alter his stance. Apparently, his defensive pose didn't rattle her any more than his scowl.

When she began to walk, he was forced to move with her or end up looking churlish. Across the room, he saw Barron smirking at him.

"I never thanked you properly for not turning me in to the authorities that night I tried to steal your book wagon."

"Barron and I have known our share of times when we could have been nabbed by the law and someone helped us," Bishop said. "Just figured it was time to pay back some good will."

"Anyway, Georgina has been very kind. In fact, everyone in Bullet has been quite lovely." She sighed in such a way Bishop couldn't help but notice how her bosom heaved.

"But there is one little thing I need your help with. You and your brother."

Bishop stiffened. "What's that?"

"My sister was kidnapped. I need your help to find her."

Get your copy of *Bishop's Bride* today or keep reading to see more books by Kathleen.

ALSO BY KATHLEEN LAWLESS

Chelsea's Choice

Lila: Rescue Me Mail Order Brides

Here Come the Brides Volume 1

Here Come the Brides Volume 2

Sweet Contemporary Romance

Frannie (Always a Bridesmaid)

Baxter (Last Man Standing)

Blue Sky Island

One Cinderella Spring

One Stolen Summer

One Fantasy Fall

One Wondrous Winter

Sweet Christmas Romance Novellas

Holly's Wish

No Groom at the Inn

Steamy Contemporary Romance
SECRET SEDUCTIONS

Her Untamed Cowboy - Book 1

Her Undercover Cowboy - Book 2

Her Unwilling Cowboy - Book 3

Who Needs a Cowboy! - Book 4

Intimate Strangers

Steamy Historical Romance

Taboo

Unmasked

Reckless Rogues - Box Set of the 2 Books

Romantic Suspense

Final Heat

Afterburn

Women's Fiction

Fabulous at Fifty

For a complete book list visit KathleenLawless.com

To be the first to hear about Kathleen's new releases, special fan pricing sales, and also receive a free book, sign up for her VIP Reader Newsletter at http://eepurl.com/bV0sb1

ABOUT THE AUTHOR

USA Today Bestselling Author, Kathleen Lawless, blames a misspent youth watching Rawhide, Maverick and Bonanza for her fascination with cowboys, which doesn't stop her from creating a wide variety of interests and occupations for her many alpha male heroes.

With nearly 50 published novels to her credit, she enjoys pushing the boundaries of traditional romance into historical romance, contemporary romance, romantic suspense and women's fiction.

She makes her home in the Pacific Northwest and loves to hear from her readers.

Sign up for Kathleen's VIP Reader Newsletter to receive updates, special giveaways and fan-priced offers. http://eepurl.com/bVosbI

KathleenLawless.com
Goodreads | BookBub
Facebook | Instagram | TikTok

goodreads.com/kathleenlawless
bookbub.com/authors/kathleen-lawless
facebook.com/kathleenlawlessnovels
instagram.com/kathleenflawless
tiktok.com/@kathleenflawless